The Killing of Jericho Slade

When Jericho Slade, the 5-year-old son of Senator Morton J. Slade, is killed in Dodge City, someone's neck is bound to get stretched. The ex-convict, Billie Flint, makes a likely suspect but when Born Gallant blunders into Dodge City and sees the innocence on the accused face, he reacts in his usual eccentric manner, snatching young Billie Flint from certain death.

Reunited with old friends, Gallant sets out to hunt down Slade's real killer but, in order to expose the truth of the murdered boy, Gallant must learn that being the hero does not always mean doing the right thing.

The Killing of Jericho Slade

Paxton Johns

A Black Horse Western

ROBERT HALE · LONDON

ISBN 978-0-7198-1308-5

Robert Hale Limited
Clerkenwell House
Clerkenwell Green
London EC1R 0HT

www.halebooks.com

Typeset by
Derek Doyle & Associates, Shaw Heath
Printed and bound in Great Britain by
CPI Antony Rowe, Chippenham and Eastbourne

PART ONE

ONE

For Born Gallant, it had been a frustrating six months since his brutally exciting stint working for William Pinkerton in Kansas City. His investigations on that world-famous detective agency's behalf had culminated in a violent encounter with the half-Indian Sunny Tancred in the Last Chance saloon at Salvation Creek. Gallant had thrived on the action, felt the blood singing through his veins, but when the gunsmoke cleared and it was all over he'd come down with an awful thump to . . . well . . . to nothing, actually. From that night on, with the scent of gunsmoke, freshly spilled blood and numerous dead bodies lingering in his nostrils but not a villain in sight, the days and weeks had been filled with dull monotony. Champing at the bit, Gallant had grown more and more restless.

He had to admit that the parting from the young

law student, Melody Lake, had also been a severe wrench, and for several reasons. The obvious one was that she was a beautiful, exciting young woman. The other was that when chance threw them together Gallant had been an aristocratic, well-spoken Englishman still feeling his way in the American West, and Melody Lake's assistance had done much more than help a green tenderfoot keep his footing on a very wobbly fence. Dark clouds had been floating across a cold moon when, for the last time, they rode into the hell-hole that was Salvation Creek. Gallant had thrust Lake behind him as he entered the Last Chance, but to no avail. Once he was inside she had taken the initiative, then resolutely stood shoulder to shoulder with Stick McCrae when the *Kansas City Star* journalist used a '73 Winchester to save Born Gallant's life.

Gallant had come across Stick McCrae's name a couple of times in the past few months. Restless, footloose, Gallant had taken to drifting through the Kansas cattle towns that had sprung up at the head of the old Chisholm trail. In Abilene, he'd stayed a night in the Bull's Head. In Ellsworth it had been the Drover's Cottage, though he did most of his drinking in Brennan's Saloon, and he'd noticed Stick's byline when perusing the *Ellsworth Reporter*. From there he'd ridden almost directly south to Wichita, poked his head briefly into Rowdy Joe's dance hall to cast an eye over the soiled doves with their painted faces and fluttering eyelashes, then eaten in a smoke-filled café where he'd again come across Stick McCrae's name – this time in the *Wichita City Eagle*. Interested but not intrigued, Gallant had slept well, risen well before dawn, then crossed the Arkansas River and headed west towards Dodge City.

That ride had taken him an unhurried three days. He rode in, more from laziness than by design, along the tracks of the Atchison, Topeka and Santa Fe Railroad. That railroad split what had once been Main Street into two. Either side had become known as Front Street and, as Gallant was well aware, the south side of those tracks was home to the red-light district and various infamous gambling and drinking joints.

Yet, observing what lay before him, he scratched his elegant golden head as much from perplexity as to soothe an itch caused by the oppressive heat, and began seriously questioning why he'd bothered coming. This was 1886, and he knew that only the previous year the laws that closed the whole of Kansas to tick-infested Texas cattle had sounded Dodge's death knell. Nevertheless, Gallant had expected more than a main street split by cold steel rails and lined on both sides by dreary business premises, crude shacks built from cheap lumber – albeit, from the looks of things, a main street that was attracting a lot of early-morning interest.

It was only as he rode his bay mare in along the north side of the railroad tracks and pulled their cloud of dust ever closer that Gallant realized what it was that was pulling buckboards and freighters to a central area. On the south side of the tracks, wagons of all kinds – even several top-buggies – were being used as stands for morbid spectators.

The object of their interest stood on the rutted dust

of the street – on a north-facing block that included Rath's general store, Chalk Beeson's Long Branch saloon, a liquor store run by George Hoover, and Fred Zimmerman's gun shop. The town carpenter had been hard at work with a saw, nails, and what leftover timber he could find. And even as a suddenly grim-faced Gallant noted the stark simplicity and sheer practicality of the construction, and the hemp rope hanging in sinister stillness above its high platform, a tight group of five men emerged from a side street not too far away and began walking briskly towards the new gallows.

The two out in front were lawmen: Gallant had them pegged as the town marshal, tall and straight, with long dark hair beneath a pearl-grey Stetson, and his chief deputy, who was red-headed, stocky and bullish. Behind them strode two men who looked like deputies sworn in for the sole purpose of ensuring that the fifth man did not break and make a run for freedom. Those four men wore their Stetsons pulled down low, shading their eyes from the sun and perhaps concealing their expressions. The six-guns at their hips hung so that a fast draw could easily be accomplished. On all four lawmen's vests the badges signifying their authority glinted in the bright sun-light.

The man walking between the two temporary deputies was bareheaded, and unarmed. His hands were bound in front of him. He stumbled as he walked, and even from a distance Gallant could see that in age he was some way short of his twenties.

A neck-tie party, staged for my benefit, Gallant

thought; they're hanging a kid to brighten my day. A dangerous smile curled his lips as the prospect of action brought the first welcome stirrings of inner excitement. But was there any need for action, for a bold attempt at rescue? For that, he realized with a sense of joy, was the outlandish notion that had set his mind racing and the hot blood once again coursing through his veins. If a young man was about to be hanged for a serious crime, and if he stood guilty as accused, then it might be regrettable, even tragic – but surely there was no reason for Gallant to interfere?

And yet. . . .

At that moment Gallant couldn't rightly say why, but the sixth sense that had served him well on India's North West frontier and helped him emerge bloodied but alive from Salvation Creek was again working over-time. Something was wrong. He wasn't sure what it was that was raising his hackles, but the whiff of injustice was strong in the air and so there was work to be done.

With a soft click of the tongue he started the thoroughbred mare across the railroad tracks and on to Front Street's south side. Then a thought struck him, and he stopped first at one of the standing wagons, a buckboard with splintered side boards and wheels with several broken spokes where an old-timer sat puffing on a clay pipe stained brown with tobacco and age.

'That kid out there with his hands tied,' Gallant said softly. 'Any idea of his name?'

'Billie Flint,' the old man snapped. 'And for what he done, God damn him to hell.'

'If he's about to be hanged,' Gallant said, 'what he

done must have been to kill another man.'

The old man sneered. 'Yeah, well, that's not what he done. If it was there'd be some room for extenuatin' circumstances dependin' on the sins or otherwise of the man he plugged.'

'And that doesn't apply in this case?'

'Damn right it don't.'

'So . . . who's in charge?'

'Liam Dolan, marshal. His deppity, Keno Lancing.'

'Thanks awfully,' Gallant said thoughtfully, and tipping a finger to his hat brim he went on his way.

Despite the impression given by the standing wagons and their occupants, the hanging was on the whole being ignored, the town going about its business. Hitch rails were lined with horses and, between the lawmen and the stationary wagons, loaded freighters and lighter buckboards were rumbling and rattling up and down the street.

A plan rapidly took shape in Gallant's mind. As the details clicked into place he moved in behind a freighter that was trundling slowly away from the general store and moving in the right direction, then pulled the mare alongside.

The chosen wagon was big, heavily loaded and rumbling slowly up the street in the direction of the gallows, its harness and tackle creaking and jingling as the load was pulled over the ruts by the team of mules. The muleskinner was a big, hunched man dressed in what appeared to Gallant to be ragged brown rags held together by frayed twine. He turned his head, spat a stream of brown tobacco juice from a mouth lost in a tangled black beard – narrowly missing

Gallant – then sneered and flicked the traces.

'If you're saving for a new suit,' Gallant said politely, resting a hand on the heaving wagon, 'I've got a shiny golden eagle that'll see you all the way to the finest gent's tailor's.'

'And I've got a scattergun nudging my boot,' the man growled, looking straight ahead, 'and for a *double* eagle I'd go so far as to kill.'

'Gosh,' Gallant said, 'wouldn't dream of anything that drastic. Just need you to heave on the traces and sort of slow those beasts down, then watch me and wait for my signal.'

'The signal being?'

'I sweep my hat off. Do a bit of a gentlemanly flourish, sure to impress. When I do that, you crack the whip and make sure you've got this heap closing on the gallows. Time it so you come close to running me down, but I make it across in front of you by the skin of my teeth.'

'And if it goes wrong?'

'My fault entirely. You pocket the cash. Can I have your name, sir?'

'Bullock,' the muleskinner said. 'Sebastian.' His black eyes glittered as he held out a hand like a scarred slab of beef. Gallant slapped a gold double eagle into the filthy palm and, as the wagon at once began perceptibly slowing, he rode off up the street. Deliberately he trotted straight on past the walking lawmen and their prisoner, glancing casually sideways at them but without showing any real interest. Then – as if sudden realization had dealt him a stunning blow – he drew rein fiercely a little way past the gallows,

11

spun his horse and, after a moment's deliberate hesitation, started back the way he had come.

The bunched men were some fifty feet away. Behind them the bearded muleskinner was holding his team back to a slow walk. Moving easily down the street, Gallant was able to study the faces of the lawmen as they approached; to look long and hard at the face of the accused man, Billie Flint.

Dammit, yes, he was young; seventeen or eighteen, perhaps small for his age but lithe and fluid of movement with a hint of cockiness in his demeanour. And Gallant had been wrong about the reasons for his unsteady gait. He'd naturally believed it was the kid's fear of dying that was weakening his muscles; the thought of the rope tightening around his neck and choking off the life-giving air draining the strength from his limbs. But this boy was like ice. His blue eyes, as he glanced in Gallant's direction, were clear and untroubled.

Further observation told Gallant the kid had stumbled because the burly men on either side, two roughs getting paid for an hour's easy work, were crowding him, jostling him unmercifully and guffawing loudly as they did so. As Gallant watched with growing anger, one of those deputies slapped the kid's head, knocking him sideways. He was met solidly by the other deputy's beefy shoulder. Again the boy stumbled at the impact, and a mocking shout from across the street had the watchers on the wagons stamping and whistling.

And while Gallant didn't allow his emotions to rage out of control, a sudden sense of outrage hardened his resolve.

Without hesitation, he took the mare at a high-stepping walk straight towards the gallows. There, he and the neck-tie party came together: five men on foot confronted by one on horseback. Gallant was quite sure the alert town marshal had been watching him ever since he overtook the party, his interest certainly quickening when Gallant turned and headed back. Now his keen eyes fastened on Gallant. As the party trudged to a dusty standstill, his hand dropped threateningly to his six-gun.

At once Gallant hoisted both hands to the sky.

'No need for that, old boy,' he said brightly. 'As you can see, I'm not carrying a weapon – "packing a gun", as you say in these parts.'

'What I see is a man who has no right to be here,' the marshal said.

'Not a right, as such,' Gallant admitted, 'but I couldn't help noticing when I rode by that the young fellow there bears a remarkable resemblance to my granddaddy.'

'To your what?' the marshal said, his eyes wide in disbelief.

'I'm not saying that he is my granddaddy,' Gallant said, waffling on, 'but that if there's a family resemblance—'

'You saying this kid's your . . . your what? Your long-lost brother, your nephew, your goddamn cousin seven times removed?'

'A closer look, a word with him,' Gallant said, 'would sort of settle it, don't you think?'

'Are you English?'

'You know, every time I open my mouth someone asks that same question,' Gallant said, grinning sheepishly, 'and I'm dashed if I know how they work it out.'

'For God's sake, Liam,' the stocky deputy said, 'send that feller the hell out of here before the kid dies of old age.'

'What's your name?'

'Flint, actually, same as his, and there's a bit of a silly first name to go with it I'd rather not—'

'Go talk to him. Make it snappy.'

'Gosh, thanks awfully,' Gallant said, gently kneeing the mare. 'And may I also thank you for tying his hands in front of him; allows him to lift them to dash away the sweat of fear, don't you know. . . .'

He continued to talk inanely of anything that came into his head as he walked the horse towards the prisoner. But while his speech and manner were reminding the lawmen that they were dealing with a typical silly ass from England's upper class, Gallant's eyes were passing a different message to Billie Flint. And the big surprise was that the message was understood. The kid might not have worked out exactly what was going to happen, but he sensed it would be extraordinary and might save his neck – and he was smart enough to wait.

'It really is very hard to believe,' Born Gallant said, closing in on the kid, 'but you're young Billie on my mater's side – aren't you?'

With that he swept off his Stetson, flung his arm across his body and, from the saddle, made a stiff bow from the waist in the kid's direction. As he did so he heard the crack of a whip, the muleskinner's horse

14

bellow, the creak of the wagon as the mules put their backs into the load. Those welcome sounds were followed by the sudden rumble of wheels on hard-packed earth.

The marshal and his stocky sidekick had moved away, and were talking as they examined the crude but serviceable gallows. The two deputies on either side of Flint were still crowding him. They were listening to all that was going on around them, watching Gallant like hawks and waiting with seething impatience. Gallant knew that men of their kind would smell danger, would react with ferocity if he gave the slightest hint of a wrong move. But his actions were so bizarre, so outlandishly foppish, they were having the desired effect: the deputies' attention was wandering, their brows were furrowed with frowns of pure disbelief and one had gone as far as removing his hat and scratching his head in bewilderment.

'Damn it, lad, this is a sad day,' Gallant said to the youngster, shovelling on gravity and dripping sentiment. 'I can do nothing for you, more's the pity, but if you're about to die then let me feel your hand in mine this one last time.'

Still leaning out of the saddle, Gallant slapped his hat back on his head and thrust out his right arm. His eyes met Billie Flint's. To Gallant's astonishment, the kid winked. Then he reached awkwardly up with his bound wrists as if to grasp the proffered hand.

Unable to suppress a grin at the lad's cheek, and knowing it was too late now to worry about giving the game away, Gallant grasped not the reaching hand but the tight binding ropes that were breaking the skin

15

and drawing blood from the prisoner's wrists. Taking a firm grip he locked his knees, tensed his muscles and, with a mighty heave, pulled the lad clear of the ground.

Flint was plucked from between the two big deputies before they had a chance to move. As the kid landed face down across the saddlehorn with a grunt followed by a whoosh of painfully expelled breath, Gallant raked the mare with his spurs. The big horse shot forward. Both deputies were bowled over by the explosion of force. One hit the ground on his back, the six-gun he had managed to claw from its holster bouncing away across the dirt. The other fell face down, kicking and spluttering in the dust.

Gallant saw none of it. As he pulled away from the deputies what he saw, out of the corner of his eye, was the heavily laden wagon bearing down on him, the bearded muleskinner up on his feet with his whip held high, lash drawn back. Closing his eyes, Gallant took the mare across the street close enough to the mule team to feel the hot, panting breath of the lead animals. The thunder of their hoofs as they rushed on up the street was deafening; the howls of anger as the big mule train came between him and the marshal and his stocky deputy were music to his ears.

Then Gallant, eyes open, was across the wide street. He took the mare at full gallop between two of the standing wagons. One hand was working the reins. The other was clinging tight to the youngster's thin cotton shirt to keep him from slipping from the horse. With the standing wagons left behind and the railroad crossed he knew he had put one more barrier between him and the furious lawmen. They were afoot. He could hear the crack of their six-guns, but he guessed that was the two enraged deputies, firing blind and for show. The marshal and his deputy wouldn't waste time with such foolishness, but by the time they had run to their horses Gallant would be a mile or more away across the prairie. If they took the time to swear in a posse, he would be halfway to Wichita – and that was more than a hundred miles away to the east.

But before then, he thought with a grim smile, he'd have to stop to let down the young man who was frantically plucking at his sleeve and complaining bitterly that on the whole he'd have preferred hanging to having a saddlehorn bore a ragged hole clear through to his backbone.

TWO

Intelligent blue eyes framed by a mass of lustrous dark hair stared questioningly at Stick McCrae.

'What was all that shooting?' Melody Lake said, dropping her pen on the desk alongside the reams of paperwork. 'A drunken cowboy doesn't seem likely, and especially not at this time of day.'

'Cowboys with cash to splash around at the end of a cattle drive would rarely be sober – but you're right, those days are gone, so there has to be another explanation.'

They were talking in a back room of the *Dodge City Times* offices. The bustle of the newspaper's main room could be heard through the closed door.

Melody cocked her head. 'You've got a secretive smirk, Stick. What's going on?'

'Born Gallant's going on, and in that old familiar, crazy, eccentric way we grew to know and love.'

'Gallant?' Melody said, her eyes widening. 'Damn it—'

Stick McCrae sucked in a breath, wagged a finger.

'Sorry,' Melody said, smiling, turning pink, 'but you

must admit his presence here warrants a mild swear word. We haven't seen him since, well, since we all rode away from the Last Chance saloon and put Salvation Creek behind us.'

'Mentioned something about a partnership, didn't he, as a parting shot?' Stick said, watching her closely. 'Famous ones being formed from less promising beginnings, something like that. Didn't quite work out that way, though.'

'So what's he done now?' Melody said abruptly.

'That kid that was heading for the gallows has been snatched from the jaws of death.'

'By Gallant?' Melody rocked back in her chair, speechless. Her eyes were bright. Behind them her thoughts were fluttering like startled birds.

'Rode in bold as brass. I was nearby, notebook at the ready for the hanging. I heard him say something about being related to Flint,' McCrae went on. 'You know the upper-class English patois he uses when he wants to create his own personal diversion – most of it from his imagination, in my opinion. Anyway, it worked the way it always does. Set those lawmen back on their heels. When they snapped out of it, Gallant had made use of a passing freighter and he and the kid were already across the railroad and heading east.'

'And now they're being pursued.'

'Yes. They're two men astride one horse, with four determined lawmen – led by Marshal Liam Dolan – not too many minutes behind them.'

'But Billie Flint is guilty.'

'Yes. I don't need to tell you the story, we wrote it up for the paper. But the essence of it was that Flint and

19

his three pals tumbled out of the bank and began a lot of wild shooting when the robbery they'd planned went badly wrong. And out of all that flying hot lead—'

'One slug screamed across the street and hit a golden-haired little boy just five years old. Killed him stone dead.'

McCrae nodded soberly.

'So why in God's name did Born Gallant decide Flint was worth rescuing from a hanging he surely deserved?'

McCrae shrugged.

'There's only one explanation,' Melody said. 'Gallant couldn't have known the full story.'

'Who that little boy was,' Stick said, 'doesn't make Flint any more or less guilty.'

'No,' Melody said, 'but it does make those fellers with shiny badges pinned to their vests more determined than ever to ensure the killer pays for his crime. Political weight has been brought to bear; their jobs are on the line.'

McCrae nodded. 'You're right, of course. When Senator Morton J. Slade paid an official visit to Dodge City, he brought with him his wife and only child. When he left, he was childless, his wife a broken woman.'

'So what the hell,' Melody said softly, 'is Born Gallant playing at?'

THREE

Five miles out of Dodge City, entering an area of thick woodland, the big bay mare stepped in a gopher hole and a foreleg snapped with the crack of a brittle branch. The horse went down head first. Billie Flint hit the ground with the suppleness of youth, but rolled awkwardly with his bound hands doing little to help. Then he was flattened as Born Gallant's full weight came crunching down on his shoulders. The big horse was kicking, struggling to rise. Flailing hoofs grazed Gallant's head. One hit his shoulder hard and deadened his left arm. He rolled out of the way, rose panting to his feet and reached down to help the kid up off the ground.

'We're in trouble,' Gallant said. 'Ironic, too: here was me rejoicing that those lawmen were afoot, and now the situation's reversed.'

Flint was supporting himself by leaning forward, hands on knees, struggling to catch his breath.

'What about the horse?' he gasped. 'You told Dolan you were unarmed. Nobody thought to leave me my six-gun, so how do we put that mare out of her misery?'

'No six-gun,' Gallant said, 'but I'm not without a

weapon. I remember once, in India, how we faced the same problem and solved it with deliberate cruelty. Bled the horse out. It was the only way.'

He reached behind him, winced as pain stabbed through his shoulder and drew his bone-handled knife from its sewn-leather sheath. He looked at the gleaming blade, the keen edge, glanced once at Billie Flint's face and the understanding in the clear blue eyes then walked towards the mare.

The artery was easily found and quickly severed. Then it was a question of Gallant and the kid holding the horse down until lack of blood brought the draining weakness that led to stillness and death. It was swift and painless, but movement they couldn't prevent meant that bright-red blood sprayed over an area of ground, and over their boots. When they rose from the dead animal they were both shaken. They spent some moments apart, gazing into the distance, controlling their emotions.

After a few minutes, Gallant called the kid over and, with a single slice of the bloody knife's razor-sharp blade, freed his wrists. Flint winced, examined the torn skin with some anger, carefully rubbed feeling back into his flesh.

Watching him absently, Gallant said, 'You know, they didn't bother with a posse. I looked back a while ago, saw four riders in the distance. They're much closer now, and I'd say we've been spotted.'

'What I've spotted is you've dropped your English accent.'

'I use that to hide my real qualities,' Gallant said, grinning.

'The only one you need now is the ability to run hard and fast.'

'Not much chance of that,' Gallant said, 'in those trees, and that's the way we must go or we'll be caught cold out here in the open.'

Flint fixed him with his clear blue eyes. 'Why did you save me from hanging?'

'I rolled out of bed feeling frisky, there was nothing better to do at the time and my sympathies always did lie with the underdog. Damn it, for the first time in a while I came alive, and even four miles out of town I couldn't see regret looming large. But five miles out my horse went down, as you know, the odds on our getting away lengthened considerably and if I'm going to flee into those woods only to go down in a hail of bullets—'

'D'you mind breaking that down into bite-sized chunks so I can chew on it?'

'Guilty or not guilty?'

'We robbed a bank, or tried to. Me and my pards – though they didn't seem to be trying too hard. But between walking in the door and running out again with gunny sacks stuffed like Thanksgiving turkeys, Marshal Liam Dolan and his deputies were closing in. There was a lot of shooting, most of it doing as much harm as Chinese firecrackers, but on the plank walk across the street a little boy went down, dead. They say it was a bullet from my gun killed him. I say they're wrong – I know they're wrong. Hell, if they can pin that on me they can just as easy make out my name's Bob Ford and I'm the man killed Jesse James.'

But Gallant was no longer listening. He had read the

truth in the kid's clear gaze, the simple honesty of his tale, and that was enough. With a final glance back at the approaching riders – now close enough for the drum of their horses' hoofs to be heard as they hammered across the hard grassland – he grabbed Flint's arm and bundled him into the woods.

As soon as they left the sunlit open prairie, Gallant knew there was a glimmer of hope. The forest stretched away before them, rising towards a ridge that could not be more than a hundred yards away. The southern edge of the woods was some thirty yards to their right – but open land was not what they wanted. Inside the woods the trees were close enough together to cause problems for men on horseback, and the tangled undergrowth that immediately began tearing at their clothes told Gallant that the lawmen would be forced to dismount. That put hunters and hunted on an equal footing – but, in Gallant's opinion, it went some way towards tipping the odds once more in his favour.

Westerners rode everywhere. Take away their horses and they were awkward critters, cursing good-naturedly as they wobbled unsteadily on boots with high heels. Billie Flint was a youngster, not yet conditioned to that life, with the strength and the fitness of youth. Gallant had been brought up in an entirely different land. He had gone from Oxford – where the blue he won at athletics had been gained in tough races across ploughed fields and through thick woods – to the British army, where fitness was a requirement and a fetish.

They could not be caught by four labouring lawmen. The only way they could be stopped, Gallant thought grimly, was by a bullet in the back.

'Split up,' Billie Flint said breathlessly, reading his thoughts. 'Give 'em two targets.'

Even as he spoke, the first shots rang out. The bullets came snicking through the branches, through the undergrowth, and were followed by the cries calling for their surrender.

'No way out,' the faint voice called over the crackling of brush, the snap of six-guns. '*Give up now, before it's too late . . . too late . . . give up. . . .*'

'We stay together,' Gallant said, tearing his sleeve free of sharp, clinging thorns. 'See, ahead—'

A twisted root caught his foot. He went down. Sharp thorns tore at his face. Broken branches were like sharpened sticks in a woodsman's bear trap, poking through his clothes as he fell, piercing his flesh. He snarled angrily, struggled to claw his way out of the tangle. He was on one knee with his other foot planted when he saw Billie Flint spin into a tree trunk, begin to slide slackly. He'd taken a bullet. His face when he turned was pale in the dappled light filtering through the leaves. Suddenly his blue eyes were awash with panic.

With a tearing and ripping of cloth Gallant came off the ground and lunged for him. He wrapped him in his arms, held him firm and upright against the tree's rough bark.

'We stay together, Billie,' he whispered into his ear, his eyes searching the down-slope. 'What I was saying, I can see that ridge up ahead. We make that and cross it, we're out of sight. On the far slope there'll be ditches, deep ones, rainwater run-offs. We'll use 'em, hide, move when we can.'

While talking he was listening to the lad's breathing, his palms exploring the youngster's clothes. In the centre of his back there was an ominous, warm wetness, quickly spreading around a hole punched through the cloth by hot lead.

But why? Why had he been shot? He and Gallant were on foot, unarmed, outnumbered. Capture was inevitable, the hanging had been postponed, not cancelled – yet the kid had been shot down in cold blood. So . . . who benefited from his death? What – if anything – was Marshal Liam Dolan anxious to keep hidden? Whose good name was he protecting?

Gallant felt the coldness of despair. He looked up the slope, saw there was another fifty yards before the ridge; looked the other way and through the trees and tangled vegetation saw the big men coming on, slow, steady, saw the glitter of their badges and guns.

'Can you walk?'

The answer was a weak, choking cough, strangled by thick liquid. Suddenly Flint's legs crumpled. His strength had leaked away with the outflow of blood pouring down his back to soak his shirt, his pants. He was a dead weight, pulling Gallant down.

Gallant drew a shaky breath. He said harshly, 'I'll carry you to safety, kid. Don't give up, one way or another—'

But the painful rasping had ceased. All the breath had been expelled from the kid's body in a final exhalation, and with it all strength, all life. Born Gallant was holding him upright, but the young man he was clutching in his arms was staring into the woods with the glassy, sightless eyes of the dead.

FOUR

He needed a horse.

Fifty yards down through the thick woodland on the far side of the ridge, Gallant was lying at the rocky bottom of one of the many deep rainwater run-offs that ran like veins from the crest. He had laid Billie Flint on the ground, crossed the skinned and bloody wrists across the motionless chest, said a brief prayer then used all his guile to thread his way through the undergrowth covering the final fifty yards up the slope without being seen.

He had heard the lawmen thrashing through the brush behind him; he had used their clumsiness and the cover of the scrub and tree trunks to mask his own movements. Once over the top he had put distance between himself and his pursuers; fighting his way downhill, even through tangled undergrowth, he was moving at twice the speed of those facing the same struggle uphill.

Then, feeling an ominous prickling at the nape of his neck and knowing that his luck couldn't hold forever, he had dived into the nearest gully. Like all

27

the others, it was choked with dead leaves. He had burrowed deep, thrashed arms and legs so that he sank lower into the rocks and loose dirt and above him the leaves floated then settled, hiding him from sight in a most natural way. He had lain there, catching his breath. The rank smell tickled his nostrils. He had no sooner ceased moving than spiders began crawling. A beetle clicked, strolled across his cheek and was flicked away as Gallant lay still, listening.

The lawmen would stop at Flint's body. They would exchange glances. The deputy who'd fired the killing shot would have his back slapped. It was possible they would decide at once that their job was done, lift the limp body and carry it back to the horses and transport the dead bank robber back to Dodge City.

Perversely, Gallant was hoping for the opposite. He wanted Liam Dolan and his men to come after him.

He got his wish.

Comatose at the bottom of his gully, stones digging like flint axe blades into his back and insects beginning to crawl inside his sticky clothes, Gallant heard the crackle of brush as the lawmen came over the ridge. They were calling to each other. Their voices were loud. The still, hot air was split by a loud crack as one of the men discharged his pistol. The slug ricocheted from a rock, there was a fading whine, and the reek of cordite hung in the air. With deliberate intent they were demonstrating their power, letting the hidden man know that he was outgunned and outnumbered four to one; that there was no escape.

Well, Gallant thought, smiling into the dusty darkness, that's as maybe – but first they had to locate him.

As if to emphasize the difficulty that would present, he heard one of the men curse softly. It was followed by a vicious crack. He had kicked out angrily at a fallen branch. There was a whirring sound, a rustling – and the branch dropped into Gallant's gully, settled in the leaves. Someone laughed, mocking the frustrated searcher with words Gallant did not catch.

'Yeah, well, seems to me we'll be here all day,' the man growled in answer, and he walked a few crackling paces. That brought him, Gallant judged, to within a few feet of where he was hiding. If this deputy's eyes had followed the branch he had kicked, he was now looking down on the leaves covering Gallant. If he leaned forward, perhaps out of frustration used the broken branch to beat at those leaves. . . .

'All day and all night, and still not get a sniff of him,' another voice called, agreeing with the first, and Gallant recognized it as belonging to the town marshal, Liam Dolan. 'That's it, pull back, lads,' he ordered. 'We've got our man. Now we'll take him back to Dodge, hang him from the noose fashioned 'specially for his neck. Let it be a lesson to all lawbreakers, let 'em see and take note of the fate awaiting rustlers, robbers, killers, anyone who breaks the law in Dodge City.'

Someone gave a mocking cheer, another man whistled and then there seemed to be a concerted rush to get back up the slope.

Deep inside his gully, Gallant stirred. Leaves rustled as he changed his position. He spat dust, and his eyes narrowed with anger.

He needed a horse now more than ever. Not to ride

hard for the Texas border, as he had intended, but to head back to Dodge City. And, having heard Dolan's hard voice utter those callous words, he needed that horse in a hurry.

Because there was now another job that needed doing.

The noise of the four men's departure had faded. They had reached the crest, and crossed over. Now they were heading back down the slope. They would stop when they reached the body of Billie Flint, take a few minutes to smoke a cigarette, gather their strength.

Born Gallant reached out with one hand to clutch at a half-buried rock, solidly embedded. He took a firm grip, then lifted a leg and wriggled over the edge of the gully. Shedding leaves like a tree in an autumn breeze, he stood up cautiously, dusted himself down, straightened the kinks out of his back and looked up the slope.

Nobody in sight.

The edge of the woods he had noted when he and Flint came in from the prairie was that same thirty yards away. Because he was facing back the way he had come, it was now over to his left. And, whereas previously the woods had offered sanctuary, a means of escape, now open ground was going to be a decided advantage.

Gallant's aim was to leave the woods and run, unseen, along their edge to where the lawmen had tethered their horses. When he walked those thirty yards through the undergrowth and stepped out into bright sunlight, he saw that the contours of the terrain were favourable.

Outside the trees, the ridge ended in a rounded grassy bluff. All the way along the edge of the trees the ground fell away steeply to a dry creek bed. With a grin that came from sheer relief, Gallant dropped those few feet down across the grass to the dry wash and commenced to jog along its length.

The clatter of his booted feet on loose dry stones seemed loud in the hot, still air, and Gallant felt a momentary twinge of unease. He estimated that the men would still be making their way back to Flint's body. Their ears would be filled with the snapping and tearing of the brush, their own harsh breathing, angry protests at the hot, sweaty work – but would that be enough to mask the noise of Gallant's progress? The creek bed was sunken, yes, but Gallant was not completely hidden. It required but a single glance in the wrong direction, at a point where the trees had thinned. . . .

It was a matter of seventy yards or so to the point where he and Flint had entered the woods. Gallant made it without the feared cries of alarm emanating from the woods, and was breathing easily. As he reached the last of the trees he could hear, ahead of him, the soft snorting of waiting horses, the jingle of harnesses.

There was also a strong smell of cigarette smoke.

Gallant slowed. He trod those last few paces with care, out of the creek bed now, and moved silently across soft grass. What he saw as he looked around the trees made him smile wryly. Liam Dolan, it seemed, had not been entirely fooled. Aware of the possibility of the two fugitives circling around to the horses, he had left one deputy on guard.

That man was now pacing impatiently near the horses, cigarette smoke trailing as he walked ten strides away from Gallant, ten strides back, all the while looking off into the woods.

Damn it, Gallant thought, now what?

He knew he was not in danger of being caught, for he could always slip away and use the creek bed as a way back to the deeper cover of the trees. But once Dolan and his men emerged from the woods carrying Flint's body, his chance of obtaining a mount would have gone up in the smoke of that accursed man's cigarette. All hope of carrying out the task he had set himself when he'd heard Dolan's cruel words would have slipped away.

And that would not do at all.

Okay, so time it down to the fraction of a second, Gallant told himself. But don't wait too long, because what you can hear now, surely, is the sound of several men blundering downhill through thick brush. They reached Flint's body, they're through talking, they're bringing him down and they're getting close. For you, my boy, time is running out – fast.

He was down on one knee, hidden by the edge of the trees, watching the deputy. Ten strides towards Gallant's position. Then the man stopped. For a moment it seemed to Gallant that the big deputy was looking straight at him. Then he looked away, lifted the cigarette, took a deep draw and turned on his heel. Again he began walking, trailing smoke, peering into the woods. One stride . . . two, three, four. . . .

And with one agile spring, Gallant was after him.

He powered himself up from a half crouch and ran lightly across the soft grass, sure of foot, as silent as a bounding cougar. Yet still the man heard him. He shot around. His eyes widened as he saw Gallant almost on top of him. He opened his mouth to yell. Gallant took off in a flat dive, his bony skull hitting the man just under the rib cage. There was the snap of bone breaking inside soft flesh. All the breath exploded from his body. He went down hard on his back, mouth gaping, chest tightly wheezing in the vain effort to suck air. Gallant was on top, straddling him. He changed position, with sure hands grasped the man's vest and rolled him over on to his front. He planted a knee hard in the small of the man's back. All his weight was concentrated on that one point. Then he leaned on the back of the man's head with both hands. Using a fierce screwing motion – one way then the other – he began to grind the man's face into the dirt.

The man's legs began drumming. The toes of his boots beat a tattoo on the ground. His lungs had emptied when Gallant's head drove into his solar plexus. Now his lungs were screaming for air, but his mouth and nose were buried in the earth. He twisted desperately. An elbow jerked wildly backwards, cracked Gallant across the bridge of the nose. His eyes filled with tears of pain. Blood began to drip on to the deputy's vest. Gallant held firm. He forced more weight down on his knee to hold the man still. Stiffening his arms, he ground the man's head harder against the soil.

'Come on, old son,' he said through gritted teeth,

'give up the ghost and let me get the hell out of here.'

He flashed a desperate look across towards the nearby woods. The danger was closer. He could hear the three men talking, their voices now much louder. Hear, too, the crunch of their boots, the crackle of undergrowth.

Under him, the deputy went limp.

Gallant squeezed his eyes shut, began counting to ten – ten seconds he couldn't afford. But he had to be sure. He hadn't wanted the man dead, but if that was what it took to put him out of action. . . .

The ten seconds up, Gallant rolled away from the still figure. He dashed the tears of pain from his eyes, the warm blood from his mouth and chin and ran for the nearest horse, a strong sorrel. There he hesitated. He knew he was pushing his luck, that time was fast running out, but he remembered a trick he had pulled when leaving the Last Chance saloon in Salvation Creek. It had worked then, and it could buy him precious time now.

The next horse was a thin paint. Gallant ducked down, again drew his knife, severed the cinch with one clean slash and gave the saddle a push. He did the same with the next two horses: bend, slice, push. The third saddle had hit the ground and he was turning away when there was a loud bellow from the woods. With a crackling of brush, a man burst into the open.

Gallant groaned. Two men carrying Flint, this one walking ahead breaking ground. He'd spotted Gallant and his unconscious colleague, seen how Gallant was consigning them all to a painful bareback ride to Dodge.

Gallant took one look at the big face contorted by rage and smiled serenely through the blood. Then he drew back his arm and with a practised whip of his forearm and wrist sent the knife spinning through the air. The whirling blade flashed in the sunlight. Gallant ran for the big sorrel.

He heard the man's grunt of pain, flashed a glance and saw him clutching the hollow of a bloodied shoulder from which the knife's hilt now protruded. But with one good arm he was still able to squeeze a trigger. The first shot cracked, but he was suffering the agony of a deep knife wound. His aim was sorely awry. The bullet thumped into the earth by Gallant's boots. As the man's breath hissed in agony and he sank limply to the ground, Gallant thought briefly of stepping across and wrenching his knife from the living flesh. Then the thought had gone, washed away by common sense. He reached the horse and flung himself into the saddle. Once astride he kicked hard with both heels. The horse started in alarm, then leaped forward with Gallant's toes fumbling for the flapping stirrups as he raced away from the woods. Shouts of anger came to him, whispers in a fading nightmare, and the six-gun shots that the lawmen fired in desperation did as much damage as dried peas shot from a child's tin shooter.

The wind was in his face, the sun on his back. Born Gallant looked to the brilliant skies and laughed in sheer delight as the big sorrel's raking strides carried him towards Dodge City. Six months of frustrating idleness had ended when a neck tic party walking a young man along a Kansas town's main street had caught his imagination and fuelled his anger. The successful rescue had ended in an innocent young man's death – for, yes, Gallant had looked into Flint's eyes and seen nothing but honesty – but for Gallant, there was much more to do.

When Liam Dolan had sworn to hang the young man's dead body from the gallows as a gruesome lesson to all lawbreakers, Gallant had been incensed. It would never happen, not if he could help it – and tied by a rawhide thong to the saddle of the horse he was riding was the rope that he needed to foil the town marshal's gruesome intentions.

FIVE

It had been a little before eight in the morning when Gallant first hit Dodge. Four hours had passed when he again crossed the iron rails and, under the blaze of the noonday sun, entered the south side of a main street that was back to normal. The standing wagons with their gaping spectators had moved on when the hanging was aborted by Gallant's impulsive intervention, the early morning rush of freight wagons had abated somewhat and, though the sidewalks were busy, there were few horsemen to be seen. As Gallant walked the big sorrel horse across the rutted thoroughfare and angled it towards the white, skeletal gallows, he was just one more rider entering town on another hot day. He attracted no attention.

Couldn't last, he thought. He'd no idea whose horse he'd commandeered, but it belonged to Dolan or one of the deputies and was likely to be a familiar sight in town. If it was Dolan's, that would be an end to it. The one horse sure to be recognized by any Dodge resident was Dolan's sorrel, and there was

37

Gallant, as large as life, forking the marshal's horse into town.

That thought brought the now accustomed grin to his face. All the way in he had been fortified by an image of Dodge City lawmen struggling across the prairie on horses without saddles. One man for certain had a knife wound in his shoulder. Another, for all Gallant knew, had died fighting for air through a mouth and nose clogged with dirt – though Gallant's past experiences across the globe suggested that he had not done nearly enough to kill a man with that deputy's toughness.

The icing on the cake, of course, was that they would now almost certainly leave Billie Flint at rest in the woods, and Marshal Liam Dolan would be forced to ride double, and bareback. That alone was enough to bring his wrath down on Gallant's head.

It was also muddled thinking, Gallant admitted. No marshal worth his salt would ride double. He would take one of the remaining horses for himself and, bareback notwithstanding, push hard for town. Gallant had been banking on reaching Dodge a long way ahead of the pursuit. The likelihood, though, was that he was rapidly being overhauled by the town marshal. There was no time to waste.

A man on foot heading along the plank walk towards the nearby livery barn glanced across at Gallant as he rode by. He lifted a hand and opened his mouth to call out, then closed it again and stopped abruptly, frowning. He walked on, but much slower than before. As Gallant cut in alongside the gallows he saw him grab a woman by the arm, gabble something into her ear and point at the marshal's horse.

Another man was emerging from Zimmerman's with a companion holding a shiny rifle. They both stopped to stare at Gallant.

'Dammit, ain't that Marshal Dolan's horse that feller's riding? Shouldn't someone head down to the jail, let 'em know?'

'Leave it to me, I'll do it.'

The man with the rifle turned, and headed back up the street.

Time was fast running out.

Gallant brought the sorrel to a halt, reached down and untied the rawhide thong holding the coiled rope. Out of the saddle, he shook the rope loose, located the loop with its slip knot. He held it awkwardly in his right hand, the rest of the rope in his left, and looked up at the gallows.

He was no cowboy. Lassoing calves and wrestling them to the lush parkland grass for branding was not a skill he had needed on his family's estate in England. But the gallows was no frisky young calf fleeing in fright to its mother. It was a crude framework of old wood held together with nails, and stood motionless against blue skies. With a deftness that took him by surprise, Gallant widened the loop, tossed it in a high arc and watched it drop neatly over the gallows.

But he was now drawing a crowd. Wagons were still trundling up and down the street, but the men and women on the plank walks were slowing and stopping, wondering what was going on. Flashing a broad grin at an old-timer in faded overalls, shrugging helplessly when the old feller called out a question, Gallant returned to the sorrel, secured the rope to the horn and stepped into the saddle.

A click of the tongue, a touch with his heels and the horse moved away to take up the rope's slack. It snapped taut. Gallant looked back, saw the gallows framework twist, then sway. As it felt the weight, the horse settled back on its haunches. Then, as if its cowpony ancestors had given it a mental prod, it took the strain and moved away again without Gallant's urging. There was a squeal that set teeth on edge as nails were drawn from green timber; a sharp crack as an upright split, from one of the watchers a hoarse yell of encouragement. Then with a despairing groan the gallows tilted, toppled and hit the dusty street with a crash.

Swiftly, as the dust rose and drifted and the gathering crowd cheered and yelled, Gallant freed the rope from the saddlehorn and wheeled the horse back towards the fallen gallows.

He might not be able to herd cows, rope steers, brand calves, but one thing Gallant could do was ride. He rode the horse at a gallows that was now nothing more than a useless timber frame enclosing a limp hangman's rope, lying on the ground but relatively undamaged. Snorting, entering into the spirit of the game, the big sorrel obeyed Gallant's skilful directions. Back and forth it went, ears flattened, eyes wild, rearing then hammering down again and again as it used its flashing front hoofs to smash the framework to firewood.

A silence settled over the street. The big horse backed off, dancing, tossing its head.

Gallant slipped down from the saddle, slapped the sorrel's sweating neck, and drew a deep, satisfied breath.

'Try hanging the kid from that, Dolan,' he murmured.

And then he froze as a voice snapped a command into the stillness.

'Step away from that sorrel, horse thief. Hoist your hands high. Make a wrong move and you're a dead man.'

For a moment Gallant did nothing, letting the harsh note of the warning fade into insignificance in the stillness. When at last he turned, he realized that he had again misjudged Dolan. The marshal had taken three men with him in pursuit of Billie Flint, but left behind his permanent deputy, Keno Lancing. While Gallant had been using the sorrel to reduce the gallows to a heap of splintered wood, Lancing had pushed his way through the watchers on the plank walk. It was his arrival that had caused the sudden hush.

Lancing stepped down into the street. There was a buzz of talk, and suddenly the crowd began to thin. The deputy was armed and dangerous; trouble hung in the air like the electric charge preceding a violent storm and people were remembering how only days before a young boy had been killed by a stray bullet.

Lancing was a stocky, red-headed figure, all muscle and sinew, his eyes glittering in an unshaven face. His clothes were dark, worn threadbare. Despite the cold gleam of the badge pinned to his vest, he exuded the chilling menace of a man who rode outside the law.

His six-gun was drawn and levelled. Inside the metal ring of the guard, his knuckle was white. He was itching to pull the trigger. If he gave in to that impulse, Gallant would have a hole in his belly clear through to his backbone.

All right, Gallant thought. Let's see what he's made of.

'Horse thief's a bit rich, old boy,' he said, walking slowly to meet the deputy. 'I found the old nag chewing grass a mile or so out of town. Was about to look for the owner, thought he might have been thrown.'

'So what are you sayin'? You just happened to be out there enjoying your morning constitutional?'

'Rather. It's been a habit of mine since I left the army. Keeps me strong in wind and limb.'

'But soft in the head,' Lancing said. 'That horse belongs to Liam Dolan. He was riding it when he went after Billie Flint. Remember? The killer you saved from hanging? And I suppose you were on your way to the jail when Dolan's horse just happened to destroy that gallows?'

Gallant grinned. To put the deputy off guard, he was holding his hands shoulder high. He continued to advance. Lancing's eyes narrowed.

Gallant walked right up to the deputy. The six-gun's muzzle bored into his lean belly.

'I could kill you, just like that,' Lancing said, his voice tight. 'Resisting arrest, you know the old story. But I know Dolan will be keen to talk to you, so what I want you to do is keep walking. I'll be right behind you. I'll direct you to the jail. You'll be locked in a cell.

42

I don't know how the hell you came by that horse, but I guarantee by the end of the day Dolan will be back in town and Billie Flint will be looking at you from the next cell.' He grinned. 'Tomorrow you'll both hang; a child killer and a horse thief. Smashing the gallows was wasted effort. All we need is a tall tree.'

'You're wrong on at least one count,' Gallant said. 'The wasted effort was saving Flint from hanging this morning, because in the end I couldn't save his life. Young Billie Flint was shot in the back. He's stone dead.'

The information caught Lancing cold. For a fraction of a second, his mind was elsewhere, the six-gun forgotten. Gallant half turned, as if obeying the instructions to walk on by. That movement pushed the gun's muzzle away from his midriff. Almost casually, he brought his right arm slashing down. The solid edge of his hand chopped the muscles of Lancing's forearm. Nerves were deadened; the six-gun fell from a hand suddenly without feeling. Gallant's left hand was there to catch it. Then he stepped back, and with an underarm swing threw the weapon up the nearest, littered alleyway.

'Sorry about that,' Gallant said. 'Damn thing must have slipped out of my hand.'

Then he ducked as Lancing, face purple with rage, clenched his fist and swung a wild haymaker that brushed Gallant's cheek as he twisted away. The force of the powerful punch hitting nothing but thin air swung the deputy completely round.

Gallant had played rugby at Oxford. The sight facing him was too good to resist. As if punting an oval ball he drew back his leg and kicked Lancing in the pants. The force of the blow drove the deputy forward, fighting to stay on his feet. One hand reached back to the injured portion of his anatomy. The other flapped wildly as he fought for balance. Then he was stumbling into the tangled mass of timber. With a roar of outrage and a crackling of wood, Keno Lancing fell face down in the shattered remains of the gallows.

It was then that the Dodge City deputy showed his mettle.

Gallant stepped back. His expression was wary. He was somewhat absently congratulating himself on a job well done while considering his next move – no horse, no weapon, the need to leave town in a hurry. Then he watched in disbelief as the lawman's frame twisted in an impossible contortion that brought him crackling and crunching to his feet and facing Gallant in a menacing crouch. Without pause, muscular thighs catapulted him out of the mess of wood. On the way he snatched up a baulk of timber two feet long and flung himself at Gallant, his eyes ablaze with murderous fury. There was a thin whistle of air as he whipped the makeshift club from behind his back in a swift, calculated swing. The hard timber blurred in a wide loop directed at Gallant's jaw.

The fierce blow was marked by the terrible crack of wood on bone. Gallant's eyes rolled, his legs folded. He flopped into the dust, went limp, groaned like an animal in pain. But just as Lancing's swing had been deliberately directed to maim or kill, so Gallant's fall was executed to deceive. With lightning reactions learned and honed on the fields of distant wars, he had ridden the terrible blow. The roll of his eyes that exposed their whites had been an act. Hidden by his body as he dropped, his right hand slapped the ground in a well-practised manoeuvre, breaking his fall.

The groan was real, unfeigned. He'd ridden the blow from the timber, but not enough to avoid injury. His mouth was awash with salty blood. A tooth wobbled to his tongue's probing and the pain in his ear was like the cruel penetration of a thin knife blade.

But the dangerous play-acting had served its purpose. Lancing, light on his feet, came at him again without haste. He was intent on finishing his man. Prone, through the thin slits of his narrowed eyes Gallant saw the man's bulk outlined darkly against dazzling sunny skies. He watched as Lancing gripped the club tightly with both hands, lifted it high over his right shoulder and turned his body. There he paused. Then, with a grunt of effort, he uncoiled, tightened the muscles in his powerful arms and shoulders and brought the club down in a chopping action as if split-ting logs.

The log he aimed for was Gallant's blond head.

With the speed of a lizard, Born Gallant twitched his lean body out of danger. He skittered lightly across the dust. The crude club bit into the dirt where an instant before his head had rested. The timber snapped. Still moving, Gallant went full circle, all the time gathering momentum. From a position on his back and with his hands firmly planted he lifted his hips, drew back his knees and drove both booted feet

45

at Lancing's belly.

The deputy's reactions were impressive, his speed deceptive. Gallant's legs were like steel pistons, fast, powerful – but the target had moved. His legs straightened, his boots grazed Lancing's hip. With no contact made, pain lanced through Gallant's knees. He flopped awkwardly down, rolled desperately as Lancing flung away the useless club and kicked at his head. His hard boot peeled a strip of bloody flesh from Gallant's cheek. Another kick exploded against Gallant's shoulder. For the second time that morning his arm went dead. He curled into a ball, tucked his legs under him, planted his feet.

Lancing came in fast, scenting blood. Gallant met him. He was a ball of lean muscle. Driven by his legs, the ball exploded upwards. The bony crown of his head drove deep under Lancing's chin. The deputy's head snapped back. He reeled away, legs buckling. Lunging after him, Gallant kicked again. He felt his boot sink into the deputy's belly. The man howled. Both hands clutching his middle, he doubled over. Gallant moved close. With a bright grin at the people on the plank walk that exposed his bloody teeth, his torn cheek, he reached out and delicately pushed the groaning deputy. Lancing fell, curled up. Then he turned his head to one side and vomited into the dust.

'Damn it all,' Gallant said, 'don't you know there are ladies over there watching your every move—'

'Born Gallant!'

An anxious voice calling from the shadows between the buildings cut through his fancy talk. Gallant became aware of the drum of hoofs on hard-packed

46

dirt. A horse was being ridden up Front Street at a fast gallop. Gallant flashed a glance towards the sound, saw that the rider had come in from the east and was crossing the railroad tracks. Then, already moving away from the groaning deputy, he looked back towards the alleyway. A dark shape moved, a hand flashed white in the deep gloom, beckoning.

With a single bound, Gallant made the plank walk. The remaining watchers parted, scattering as he pushed through with a muttered, 'I do beg your pardon,' and turned to run for the alleyway. The milling crowd was his camouflage, a mass of humanity in the midst of which Gallant was just another uniden-tifiable shape as a big man riding bareback dragged a billowing plume of dust towards the ruins of the gallows and there pulled his mount to a sliding halt alongside Lancing.

Then Gallant saw no more. He skipped through the last of the crowd and leaped down from the plank walk into the gloom of the alleyway that cut between the high buildings. In his bloody nostrils there was the stink of rubbish, of rotting food and the reek of rabid cats. Then his arm was grasped as a man stepped out of the shadows. Roughly, he was bundled through a doorway into deeper darkness, and now the smell was of lamp oil and cigarettes, of beer and stale perfume. He expected to enter a large, long barroom, for he knew without thought that he had been dragged through a side entrance and into the building that was the Long Branch saloon. Instead he was pulled into a passageway that led to the rear of the premises, then on to a flight of bare, flimsy stairs up which he and his

47

rescuer clattered noisily, and so along another passageway that doubled back towards the front of the building where a window overlooking the street let in a flood of bright sunlight.

Breathing hard, he was pushed through a door that opened at their approach, then slammed to behind them.

'Well, knock me down with a feather,' Gallant said softly, 'if it isn't the lovely Melody Lake.'

SIX

Stick McCrae had lit a cigarette and was lounging to one side of the window, holding back the filthy net curtains and watching and listening to what was going on below him on Front Street. He was a tall, spare young man with mid-brown hair, an ordinary face and ink-stained fingers. Dressed in a white shirt with arm bands and dark serge trousers, he looked like a typical small-town newspaper worker. Yet, looking at the man's confident demeanour, Gallant couldn't rid himself of the image of this same Stick McCrae holding a '73 Winchester across his knees in a Kansas City hotel room as shabby as the one in which they were now hiding. And coolly and without a change of expression threatening Gallant with the gleaming repeating rifle.

Melody Lake was watching Gallant with concern. He was favouring his shoulder. His nose was swollen and the ripped flesh on his cheek was leaking watery blood.

He shook memories out of his head, and raised a questioning eyebrow.

'What in heaven's name are you doing in Dodge City?'

'I moved here when Stick left the *Kansas City Star*. I write copy for the *Times*, which everyone assures me is brilliant.'

'But isn't it insanely boring?'

'If I was confined to an office here in Dodge, that might be true,' Melody said. 'But I get out a lot. For example, in the next couple of days I'm riding to Buck Creek. An Irishman has taken over the Drop Inn saloon. I'm going to talk to him.'

'Lucky fellow,' Gallant said, grinning then wincing as pain shot through his cheek. 'Well, I'm sure you'll pick his brains and come up with a good story, but weren't you studying hard to be a lawyer?'

Melody, sitting comfortably on a bed with a rock-hard mattress in that dingy room above the Long Branch's barroom, smiled ruefully.

'Indeed I was. But then I stood in the shadows and watched a fair-haired young man from England play dangerous games with two gunmen in a bar in Salvation Creek. After that, how could anything ever be the same again?'

'But Melody, Melody,' Gallant said softly, 'you were close to embarking on a career that would have set you up for life. How could you walk away from that?'

'I'm surprised you can ask that question with a straight face, Gallant. Weren't you heir to an estate in England? And didn't you inherit one day, and give it all away the next?'

'To my sister,' Gallant said. 'You've not known me for long but you've had a chance to judge my character so

50

you must know I wasn't cut out to be a country squire.' He waggled his eyebrows. 'Graduated from Oxford, went straight into the army and had a whale of a time playing soldier in faraway places hot enough to fry eggs on rocks. And then. . . . Well, back in England Father had died and I remembered this Scottish friend of his called Pinkerton who'd started a detective agency over here, and after that—'

'You can't keep your nose out of trouble,' said Stick McCrae.

'It's not exactly a habit,' Gallant said. 'Not yet, anyway, although crossing swords with the West's bad boys has its attractions.' He grinned. 'The fact is I'm a bit like those Pinkertons. I can't tolerate injustice, and if I see a wrong I simply have to put it right.'

'Those Scottish brothers ran a business because they needed money. You gave up property, but pocketed a lot of cash,' Melody pointed out.

Stick McCrae was shaking his head.

'Billie Flint was a robber who would have been hard pressed to break into his kid brother's piggy bank. But in his last desperate attempt to get rich he blazed away with his six-gun and killed an innocent little boy. So where's the injustice? Which wrong were you attempting to put right?'

'The lad told me his story. How d'you know it was his bullet killed that child?'

McCrae hesitated, then flashed a look at Melody. 'How do we know?'

She frowned thoughtfully, touched her long dark hair.

'Well, Billie was left stranded outside the bank when

51

his horse bolted. There was some fierce gunplay, a lot of wild shooting. One of the other robbers, a Mexican, hung back and tried to drag Billie on to his horse, but the law was closing in fast and it came to nothing. It was all over when three of the bank robbers hightailed it, empty-handed, and Dolan arrested Billie and carted him off to jail. The next we heard was a fierce hammering as the gallows went up, and the news that Billie Flint was to be hanged for murder.'

'No trial?'

McCrae shook his head.

'So Billie Flint was convicted on Dolan's say-so.'

'It looks that way,' McCrae said. 'And it's easy to see why.'

'We did a short, respectful piece about the young boy that died,' Melody said. 'Again, it's not hard to see why the editor wanted it, considering who the boy was.'

Gallant rolled his eyes. 'So, come on, who was he?'

'His name was Jericho Slade. He was the 5-year-old son of Senator Morton J. Slade. Slade hails from Wichita, but spends a lot of time in Washington. He was here with his wife on an unofficial visit.'

'Unofficial means what, exactly? He was here to visit somebody?'

'For personal talks with Liam Dolan,' McCrae said.

'The *marshal*! What the hell—?'

'Dolan is ambitious. Some months ago the senator needed an escort on a train journey through the Dakota badlands. Dolan was the man in charge.' McCrae shrugged. 'Slade subsequently offered Dolan a permanent job on his staff. His visit here was to work out the details.'

'Dolan, in charge of security,' Gallant said, nodding. 'And on that unofficial visit, the senator's son is shot dead. Hell, no wonder Dolan went after Billie Flint.'

'But the hanging didn't happen, did it?' McCrae said, and he eased back from the window and looked hard at Gallant.

'No, it didn't,' Gallant said, 'and it never will. I snatched the kid from the neck-tie party and got him as far as some timber country lying to the east. Dolan and his men caught up with us there. Billie was shot in the back, and if I was a betting man I'd put money on Dolan pulling the trigger.'

'So Billie Flint's dead?' Melody said softly.

'Died in my arms. Shortly after that I overheard Dolan saying he was going to hang the kid, dead or alive, as a lesson to all lawbreakers.'

McCrae swore softly. 'Which explains why you came tearing back to town on Dolan's sorrel and went berserk.'

He was back watching the street. Despite his obvious anger at hearing Dolan's intentions, his manner was relaxed, his attention wandering.

'Nothing much happening out there?' Gallant suggested.

McCrae shook his head. 'All quiet. Dolan's taken his horse to the stable, and I guess he'll head down to the jail. Mingling with the crowd got you clear, so he's being realistic. You've either left town already, or you're in hiding. Why search for you when sooner or later you'll be forced to show your face?'

'One that's too easily recognized,' Melody said.

'Sadly, yes; when I rode brazenly up to that neck-tie party I was banking on getting clear for good,' Gallant said with a rueful smile. 'Didn't expect to see any of 'em again and, looked at that way, riding back into town was well-intentioned but not too clever. Could have walked away through those woods. Instead, I've stuck my head back in the noose, so to speak.' He hesitated, thought over what he'd just said. 'You've been watching the street, Stick,' he said. 'Dolan's pards showed up yet? Three fellers riding bareback, two of them the worse for wear, clothing bloodstained, trouble breathing – that sort of thing?'

Melody looked quickly at him, her blue eyes wide. Gallant winked.

McCrae said, 'No, I've not seen 'em.'

'So. . . .'

'Maybe they had orders to bury Billie Flint in the woods,' Melody suggested.

Gallant was still thinking. With Melody occupying the bed, he had been making do with the hard chair next to the washstand. Now he stood up, tall, straight, fair hair tousled, and began to pace restlessly. Then he stopped, shook his head.

'I don't think Dolan would want 'em to do that.'

'I agree,' McCrae said. 'What I think is, those deputies have taken Billie home.'

'We wrote a couple of paragraphs about Billie and his parents,' Melody said. 'Billie's father's also well known. His name's Guthrie Flint. He's big in small-town politics.'

'And where's home?'

'Wichita. He and his wife live in a big house to the south of the town. He's not as important as Slade, obviously, but hailing from the same town the two men are close friends.'

'Intriguing,' Gallant said. 'Dolan's promising career is cut short when, outside the bank, Guthrie Flint's son Billie shoots dead Jericho Slade, his friend's golden-haired little son. And then Dolan's faced with the unenviable task of stringing up the senator's friend's son. Damn it, if you made up a story like that for the paper, your editor would laugh himself sick.'

'The spread roughly southeast of those woods where Billie died is owned by a rancher called Franklin Land,' McRae said. 'The deputies could make for Land's place, two men riding double and another with Billie's dead body belly down. Franklin Land owes Dolan favours. Once he knows what's going on he'll tell Dolan's men to leave the horses, and he'll give 'em the use of a buckboard that'll get them to Wichita.'

Melody was frowning. 'It's all plausible, but why would Dolan put his men to all this trouble? Surely what we said first is the easy way, the sensible way: bury the kid in the woods.'

'Morton Slade knows Billie Flint shot his son,' McCrae said. He'd lit another cigarette, and was smoking furiously as he talked. 'However, Slade and his wife left town the same day, so that's *all* he knows. Dolan's already in bad with Slade, and he's going to look worse when Slade finds out Billie Flint escaped.'

'Indeed he is,' Gallant agreed. 'So if Dolan sends Billie home to his pa, then succeeds in capturing me

– the man who helped Billie escape – he'll have gone a little way to restoring his reputation.'

Melody nodded. 'And he can do more, can't he? Billie's dead, and the dead can't talk. Dolan can now cast blame for that little boy's death elsewhere: Billie was a mistake; he'll go after one of the other robbers.'

'Anyone out there on the street at that time, blazing away with a six-gun, could have downed that boy,' Gallant said. 'Dolan thought it was Billie but he can admit to Slade that, given more time, he's realized his mistake.' He nodded thoughtfully. 'He could be right, too, because sure as hell I don't believe Billie was guilty. Worked like that, Dolan becomes the thinking man's lawman. He's got me, then he goes out hunting and comes back with the man who shot Slade's son.'

'What about Billie's death?' Melody said. 'He was shot in the back. Another politician's son. Dolan dare not take responsibility. He and his men must be blameless.'

'I have a horrible feeling about that,' Born Gallant said, crossing to the window and gazing out on the sunlit street.

'Only natural,' McCrae said. 'The other man present when Billie Flint died was a whole lot closer to the kid than any of those deputies. The death of Slade's boy fuelled a lot of anger in Dodge. Who's to say a gunslinger wasn't hired to snatch Flint and mete out a different and very personal kind of rough justice?'

'Gunslinger?' Gallant said, turning and smiling crookedly. 'Me?'

Melody, appalled, was nodding furiously. 'I think

Stick's on to something. Liam Dolan thinks fast. I can see that idea appealing to him.'

'Well, I know of one excellent way of finding out if Stick's right,' Gallant said. 'As soon as I leave this rotten little room I'll walk to the nearest stable, buy me a horse and rig and make the long ride to Wichita to talk to Guthrie Flint.'

McCrae grimaced. 'You think that's wise?'

'A cold-blooded killer,' Gallant said, 'fears no man.'

'In that case,' McCrae said, as Melody put a hand to her mouth to hide a smile, 'you should also stop at Zimmerman's and buy yourself a Colt .45, a rifle, and boxes of shells for both.'

Gallant shook his head. 'Can't do. I'll be leaving here under cover of darkness. Zimmerman will be tucked up at home keeping his wife awake with his snores. What about you? Can you help me out?'

'Certainly. I'll provide the weapons. And here's another suggestion you should act on: take somebody with wisdom and local knowledge along to watch your back.'

'Got anyone in mind?' Gallant asked innocently.

But all Stick McCrae did was grin and head for the door.

PART TWO

SEVEN

Born Gallant and Stick McCrae rode out of the limit-less expanse of prairie to the west of Wichita with midnight long gone and a cold moon high in cloud-less skies adding a glistening sheen to grass, sage, cottonwoods and willows wet from recent rain. With a soft sigh that could have signified anything, including boredom, Gallant drew rein under a dripping canopy of grey leaves and waited for McCrae to join him.

Gallant was riding a roan mare. Two days before, shortly after following Stick McCrae from the room above the Long Branch, Melody Lake had pressed silver coins into the gnarled hand of the old hostler and coolly led the horse out of the front entrance to Dodge City's main stable. Under the suspicious gaze of Marshal Liam Dolan – to whom she had waved cheer-fully – she had mounted, then ridden past the jail and out to her adobe and timber cottage sheltered by a thick grove of aspens on the city's outskirts.

Later that evening Stick McCrae had left the Dodge City's *Times* office, collected an assortment of weapons from his home and joined Melody Lake. Later still, under cover of darkness, Gallant had left the room above the Long Branch, traversed the dusty passage-ways and slipped out into the night. On foot, he had hugged the city's shadows and made it without inci-dent to Melody's cottage.

There they had all eaten a cold supper. Shortly after that the two men had bidden farewell to Melody, who was downcast at being left behind but looking forward to her own ride to Buck Creek. Armed, and with rations in their saddlebags sufficient for several days, they had crossed the iron rails bisecting Front Street and pushed their horses hard as far as the woods where Billie Flint had died. From that point, consid-ering themselves safe from pursuit, they had moderated their pace and ridden confidently across Franklin Land's property with the lights of his big ranch house some half-mile distant.

Now Gallant was looking at another house belong-ing to a man of some importance, surprisingly well lit at such a late hour.

'That it ahead? Those lights? If so, there's activity I can't make out too well from here.'

Gallant was looking down a long, raking slope that would eventually take them all the way in to Wichita if they continued their ride. But a little way to the north the house he had spotted was set in the lee of another grassy rise, a ghostly shape bathed by the chill moon.

Softening that cold image, warm, homely lamplight

glowed in the windows of its lower floors. In the spa-
cious fenced yard that stretched down the slope to a
massive wooden gate – standing open – Gallant could
see men moving, a wagon of some kind, that same
moonlight glinting on weapons of steel.

'That's Flint's house,' Stick McCrae confirmed.
'And if that's the buckboard Franklin Land loaned
those deputies, we could be set for a confrontation.
May get a chance to exercise your trigger finger,
baptize your new weapons with fire. You happy with
that?'

McCrae, it seemed, stored in his small house a
weapon for every occasion, and sufficient to equip an
army. The butt of an old Henry rifle handed over by
the journalist in Melody's cottage now jutted from
Gallant's saddle sheath. A gun-belt around his waist
sagged with the weight of a Colt six-gun almost as old
as the Henry but well used and freshly oiled, and a
replacement knife was in the sheath at the small of his
back.

'That buckboard theory of yours was pure conjec-
ture,' Gallant pointed out.

'Backed up now by what we see, though, wouldn't
you say?'

'All I see is a buckboard that's about to move out of
a yard.'

McCrae snorted. 'That's no working ranch we're
looking at. It's a private house, so activity of that kind,
at this time of night, has to be suspect.'

'Point taken,' Gallant murmured, saddle creaking as
he shifted position. 'Let's assume you're right: that buckboard was carrying Billie Flint's body, the handover's

been done and Flint's grief-stricken, or angry enough to chew rocks and spit out the bits.'

'So what do we do now?' McCrae said. 'Ride up to the house and face Flint's wrath?'

'Facing him's been my intention all along. What we're after is information on those bank robbers. He's the father of one of them, so who better to ask?'

There was enough shelter under the cottonwoods for Gallant and McCrae to ease back into the dripping shadows and watch the unsuspecting deputies rattle by in the rickety buckboard. The deputies' presence there – two of them clearly carrying wounds – proved beyond doubt that McCrae had been right: the buckboard had been used to transport the dead body of Billie Flint. And it was with the realization that Guthrie Flint's reaction to their arrival would at the very least be unpredictable that they rode out of the trees and took their tired horses swishing through long wet grass and through the house's wooden gate to splash across the slick mud of the yard to the big house.

Lamplight still glowed in the downstairs rooms. The front door was open, and a well-lit hallway could be glimpsed, though only just; a man's figure was blocking most of the opening. His face was entirely in shadow, but his huge frame was suggestive of raw power. Gallant noted at once that he was carrying a shotgun. Its double barrels, glinting in the warm light, spelled danger. It was held casually by the big man, but Gallant knew that a blast from both barrels would tear him apart and put him down to die bloodily.

McCrae was ahead of him. Seeing the shotgun

twitch in the big man's hands, Gallant pulled the journalist back by the slack of his damp vest. Jaw tight, looking high to get a glimpse of the man's eyes – for the eyes will always betray a man's carefully guarded intentions the instant before he acts – he walked boldly up to the door.

Where he was brought to an abrupt halt.

'Born Gallant?' the man said, in a voice too soft and gentle for his size and raw power.

'Spot on, first time,' Gallant said, 'though it beats me how you worked it out. Second sight, was it? You some sort of witch doctor, tribal medicine man? Or was it a wild guess? Surely nobody would pluck a name like mine out of their hat?'

'I'm Guthrie Flint. By the sounds of it, you'd be happy to lull me to sleep with inanities,' the big man said, a hint of amusement in his voice. 'However, there are things to be discussed that need my full, wide-awake attention. Why don't you and your friend come inside, and we'll partake of some fine whiskey while getting down to business?'

'You won't recall the occasion,' Guthrie Flint said, 'but I caught sight of you one afternoon when you were deep in conversation with Bill Pinkerton. Bill's a good friend of mine. Speaks very highly of you. That's why I knew those badged oafs from Dodge City who have just left were talking claptrap when they called you a cold-blooded killer. They swore you were some kind of vigilante, paid to snatch Billie, take him to those woods and mete out some kind of justice. Who the hell would do that, I asked them, when hanging a man

62

legally is justice, a shot in the back pure murder? They couldn't answer, because what they were suggesting was balderdash.'

'Not entirely. I was in those woods. I did see your boy die.'

'But you saved him from hanging – that much they conceded. And you didn't kill that boy, because if you were a guilty man I'd see it in your eyes.' Flint, as if knowing he'd caught out Gallant at his own game, half smiled as he cocked his head. 'And now?' he said. 'Well, now you're here – but to do what, exactly?'

Earlier on he had broken the seal on a bottle of imported whiskey and taken three glasses from a handsome oak cabinet. It was now half an hour since he'd invited Gallant and McCrae into his home. Slumped in a deep easy chair, feet on a sheepskin rug, McCrae looked half asleep. Gallant guessed that was a pose, for from time to time he noticed the glint of watchful eyes behind the slitted lids.

The room was expensively furnished, lit by several ornate oil lamps, and thick rugs were scattered over the wooden floor. Flint was as big as he'd looked in the doorway, grey hair grizzled, a paunch testing the buttons of his white shirt of a size to match his build. His wife, he'd told them, was asleep upstairs, so they'd kept their voices down. But it had all been small talk. Now, something more was required.

'Your son's body was brought here not an hour ago,' Gallant said carefully.

'And is now at rest on a long table in the library. Tastefully draped.'

'Yet since we began talking I've not seen a glimmer

of emotion when your boy's name has been mentioned. Not once in all that time have I heard you call him your son.'

'There's very little emotion because I hardly knew him. He was not my son. I married his young widowed mother a year ago. Billie came along as baggage. He took my name – happened to like the sound of it – but all his mother's entreaties couldn't persuade him to live in my house.'

'If he was contemplating mixing with a wild bunch,' Gallant said, 'I could see how Flint would have a certain cachet.'

'He didn't realize he needed more than a fancy name to cut the mustard,' Flint said bluntly. 'He was out of his depth. Rode south, got in with a bunch of ruffians, hard fellers with jail time and a trail of dead men behind 'em. Ended up as the green kid ordered to hold the horses out in the street while those men with guns robbed banks.'

'Talking of names,' Gallant said, 'what do they call themselves?'

'There you've got me beat. Sean and Patrick Brannigan are the bad eggs of the bunch, so I guess it could be the Brannigans. Or maybe the Brannigan Boys.'

'Which sort of brings us to the nub,' Gallant said.

Flint nodded slowly, the smile gone. 'The Brannigans rode into Dodge, bold as brass. Billie was accused of shooting down a tow-headed boy just five years old when the bank robbery went badly wrong.'

'Son of Morton J. Slade. A close friend of yours.'

'And Mort couldn't believe Billie did it. *Wouldn't*

64

believe it – for which I thanked him.' He shook his head. 'Those deputies accused you of killing Billie.'

'Dolan must have told them what to say before they split up and he rode back to Dodge. But I was there, in those woods, and Billie was shot dead by one of those deputies, or by Dolan himself.'

'As for the other,' Flint added, 'Marshal Liam Dolan is now saying Billie's bullet didn't kill the boy.'

Gallant shook his head. 'They kill him, then say he wasn't guilty? What the hell is Dolan playing at?'

'Well, if Billie's innocent, somewhere out there there's a guilty man laughing up his sleeve.'

Stick McCrae stirred, fully opened his eyes.

'Then God help him.'

Flint grinned. 'Gallant's after him. Is that what you mean?'

'An English blue-blood hits the trail. Enough to make any desperado shake in his boots,' McCrae said, yawning insolently.

'The shaking could be from laughter,' Gallant said amiably.

'Ah, but the affair that was terminated in Salvation Creek will forever be appended when your name comes up in talk around camp-fires,' Flint said, draining his glass and fixing Gallant with a pensive gaze. 'If those boys holed up on the old Travis spread hear you're after them – if that killer knows you're hot on the scent . . . well, I won't say they'll be shaking in their worn-down boots, but they'll spend a lot of nervous time looking over their shoulders.'

McCrae, up on his feet now and stretching out the kinks in his lean frame, looked quickly at a suddenly alert Gallant.

'Travis spread,' Gallant said softly. 'All you've given me is a name that rolled off the tongue and carried on straight out of the door. Can you be more precise?'

'Forty miles south of here. On flat land near a small settlement called Buck Creek. Sage, grass, lot of scrub, trees here and there – aspens, cottonwoods, mesquite. Big old house, run down but solid, part logs, part flat boards, with a yard, broken fences and a falling-down windmill sucking up good clear water. Sprawling somewhat because old Travis, when he worked it, built a room or lean-to on almost every year.' Flint grinned. 'I guess that's exaggerating a mite; he was there for close on thirty but those additions make it difficult for a stranger to find his way through a boxy maze.'

'Got to get in, first,' Gallant said. 'A house of any kind on an expanse of flat prairie with little cover is difficult to approach in daylight. If it's solid, that makes it worse. And those boys are going to be as jumpy as day-old fleas.'

'Then go in at night,' Flint said bluntly.

McCrae was puzzled. 'If they're known to hole up at this Travis place,' he said, 'why haven't they been arrested?'

Flint shook his head. 'I've no idea. But after what happened in Dodge, if anyone should be after them it's Marshal Liam Dolan.'

'So why isn't he?'

'That's something you'll have to ask Dolan your-self,' Flint said, rising from his chair and placing his empty glass on the table to bring the discussion to a close. 'Always supposing,' he said, 'that you're in a fit state to do so when – or should I say if? – you ride away from the Travis place.'

EIGHT

They spent the night in a straw-lined loft above the barn behind Guthrie Flint's house. Flint himself cooked them a breakfast of fried eggs and salty ham, watched as they washed it down with several cups of black coffee, his shadow cast large by the bright, early-morning sun streaming through the kitchen's east-facing window. When Gallant and McCrae rode away from the house, they were comfortably well fed. They also had the councillor's good wishes ringing in their ears.

Gallant had taken Flint's almost throwaway advice to heart: approaching enemy positions in full darkness was a tactic he had often used as an army officer serving on the Indian subcontinent. Advancing bare naked across open ground in broad daylight, as he put it to McCrae, would expose them to a withering fire laid down by trigger-happy outlaws safe behind the Travis house's log walls.

So, with the decision to go in at night made soon after leaving Flint's place, they rode their horses at a pace calculated to get them to the Brannigans' spread when the sun was well down in the west. The terrain was easy, undulating prairie criss-crossed here and there by the wide cattle trails coming out of Texas, most too recently used to be overgrown.

In the end it was one of these – possibly the Chisholm trail, according to McCrae – that led them to a landmark Flint had described: a rocky bluff topped with pines that, seen against the night skies, would look like an Indian in full headdress. That bluff, he said – Lone Cree Ridge – was midway between Buck Creek and the Brannigan place. Buck Creek was to the west. Point their mounts' noses at the eastern skies, and after a mile or so they'd come up behind the Travis spread.

Several hours later, they had the house in their sights.

They drew rein at the side of the broad cattle trail, and quenched their thirst from canvas water pouches. Two hundred yards away, the rear walls of the house were painted red by the setting sun. The lurid light was reflected dazzlingly from windows of unbroken glass – something McCrae remarked on with surprise – and an ancient stone chimney reared into the fading light. The blades of the windmill in the front yard, and a little of its rickety structure, could be seen above the roof of the house. There appeared to be just the one back door. It was standing open.

'If we make our move before full dark instead of after,' Gallant mused, eyeing that dark opening, 'they'll have the sun in their eyes – if they're sober enough to keep watch, that is. My guess is they're drunk on mescal, sitting smoking evil cheroots and slapping greasy playing cards on a filthy table. If I'm right, we can walk straight in through that open door and catch 'em with their pants down.'

'Before dark means now,' McCrae said, easing his six-gun. 'Leave it any longer the sun will be down below the horizon.'

Gallant grinned across at him. 'Never did believe in hanging about,' he said. 'Like a visit to the dentist, imagination plays havoc with the nerves; very rarely matches reality.'

The trees Flint had mentioned as being common to the region were mostly isolated, and stunted by long exposure to the burning sun. But a stand of healthy willows and cottonwoods ran east to west along a small creek some fifty yards to the north of the house, and it was towards these that Gallant led the way. As they drew closer they were forced to splash their horses across the stony bed of the creek, which bent a little to the south in front of them. Once up the opposite bank, they rode through the trees and then alongside them towards the house in the long shadows cast by the last rays of the setting sun.

'Almost too easy,' Gallant said softly.

'Sensible thing to do was ride up to the front door. Done this way announces bad intentions—'

McCrae broke off as Gallant leaned across to grab his arm.

'There,' he said, pointing ahead. 'Dammit, Stick, that back door's open 'cause there's a privy in those trees and there's a man—'

The shot that cut him off in mid-sentence was a blaze of light followed by the brittle crack of the exploding cartridge. It was almost drowned as the man running from the wooden privy tucked into the woods began yelling like a crazy Indian. He had long black hair, wore a dirty grey undershirt and was clutching his trousers with one hand. Screaming a warning that a goddamn posse was closing in, he sprinted towards the dark doorway. He was shooting wildly as he ran. Bullets snicked through the trees over Gallant's head, kicked dirt in front of the frightened horses.

Backing into the trees, Gallant and McCrae watched the panicked outlaw reach the house and disappear into the black maw of the interior. Gallant was cursing in a gentlemanly way. The element of surprise had been snatched from them by the unfortunate positioning of a crude outhouse, the timing of one man's call of nature.

'We've blocked that back-door getaway,' McCrae said bitterly, 'only for them to leave by the front door.'

'Or maybe not,' Gallant said. He was listening hard while surveying the immediate area. Held lightly under slack reins his nervous roan mare was pivoting at the edge of the trees, twitching its tail, its ears pricked. 'Their horses are in that pole corral off to the right side of the house,' Gallant went on, eyes busy. 'See it, over there? Badly placed. Too much open ground for them to cross; hurried saddling to do if they make it to the corral. And that's the fear that'll be in their drink-addled minds: trying to do the impossible under a hail of bullets.'

'Then they'll stay where they are, and make it easy for us,' McCrae said, and looked at Gallant.

Gallant grinned.

'Intrepid Dodge City journalist comes up with a clever idea. Right?'

'Covered by these trees,' McCrae said thoughtfully, 'I'll work my way around to a position on the north side of the house. Once I'm settled under cover, I'll spray the house with bullets using rifle and six-gun. That will convince them the posse's split, and storming the house from two directions.'

He'd moved off before Gallant could reply. Gallant watched him weave his horse through the trees. Then he became as one with the woods in the deepening gloom of nightfall. In the velvet silence, saddle leather creaked, metal tinkled and brush crackled under McCrae's mount's hoofs. If the outlaws had ears sharp enough to catch those sounds, the plan would be on its way to working: the men holed up in the Travis house would, even through an alcoholic haze, mentally trace the direction of those sounds and be at once alerted to an imminent attack from the north.

In the stillness of the night the first report from McCrae's rifle assailed Gallant's ears like the thunderous boom of a small cannon. He listened as McCrae triggered the long gun four more times, then switched to his pistol and fired a volley with the smaller weapon – clearly from a different position. At once, from the windows on the north side of the house, there came a furious burst of answering gunfire.

Leaving his horse tethered, Gallant moved out of the trees and set off on foot across the wet grass.

He ran like the wind, blond hair flying, the old Colt

six-gun cocked and ready in his right hand. He stayed close to the trees, ran swiftly through their shadows and the stench drifting from the privy, then cut across at an angle that brought him up against the wall of the house close to the back door. He was breathing easily. If his rapid approach had created the merest whisper of sound, it had been drowned by the rattle of gunfire.

With his back flat against the wall, Gallant knew the noise of the battle raging on the other side of the house was both a blessing and a curse. Try as he might, he could not hope to catch furtive sounds that might warn him of a man lurking in the dark interior beyond the open back door.

'Nothing for it,' Gallant muttered, 'but to take the jolly old bull by the horns.' Sucking in a deep, sweet breath of cool night air, he inched his way along the wall. He reached out, gripped the door jamb with his left hand. Paused. Then, using the muscles of that arm to catapult himself forward, he exploded in through the doorway. He hit the open door hard with his shoulder. It banged against the wall, rebounded, hit him in the face. As he instinctively recoiled, his ankles crossed and he fell flat on his back.

It saved his life.

Out of the Stygian darkness a muzzle flash bloomed vivid red, dazzling white. In the confined space the sound of several rapidly snapped shots was deafening. The speed of their execution told Gallant, sprawled but holding tight to his six-gun, that in the manner of a gunslinger the outlaw was holding the trigger back and fanning the hammer.

Then a sudden silence fell over him.

His attacker had fanned the hammer wildly, ineffectively and without ceasing. Then it clicked on an empty chamber. Grasping the empty weapon by its hot barrel, he uttered an obscene curse, dropped on Gallant and began chopping at his head.

Dammit, Gallant thought, this is getting to be a habit.

The infuriating notion flashed through his mind like a lightning bolt. It was followed by an eruption of righteous anger. Struggling to bring his own pistol into action, instinct was enabling him to evade the violent blows. Twisting, jerking, he felt the butt of the weapon graze his scarred cheek, heard the crack as it slammed down again to hit the hard dirt floor next to his ear.

The man was straddling Gallant. In the fading light admitted by the now half-open door Gallant could see the lank black hair, the dirty undershirt, smell the acrid reek of stale sweat. The outlaw's black eyes glittered. His lips were drawn back in a frustrated snarl. His body twisted. He pulled back, his arm raised high preparatory to another vicious blow.

That freed Gallant's right arm.

With the speed of a striking rattlesnake, he rammed the muzzle of his six-gun under the outlaw's chin and pulled the trigger. There was a liquid splat. Blood and brains splashed against the sagging ceiling. The man toppled backwards. Gallant bucked, then kicked the dead body clear and scrambled to his feet.

He was in a small back room. Windowless, there was nevertheless enough dim light for him to see that it was bare of furniture and littered with broken crates, newspapers brown with age, empty liquor jugs.

And one dead body. And a bloodstained ceiling that intermittently dripped gore.

Gallant smiled grimly. In front of him was a closed door leading to the interior of the house. He stepped over the dead outlaw. Four paces took him across the room. A bottle without a neck rolled under his foot. He kicked back absently. The broken glass cracked wetly against the outlaw's ruined skull as Gallant pressed his ear to the door's heavy oak panels.

On the other side of the house gunfire still crackled, but sporadically. There was an impasse, a stand-off. McCrae had done his job. He had drawn the main force away to allow Gallant's entry. Now, comfortably settled under woodland cover, he awaited developments.

Gallant's fight with the outlaw had started explosively, reached its bloody climax in seconds. The heavy oak door had prevented the noise of the brief struggle from reaching outlaw ears dulled by the noise of battle. Confident that the outlaws facing McCrae were unaware of his assault on the rear of the house, Gallant pulled the door open and slipped through into an interior passageway.

And now there was a glimmer of yellow light.

The dusty passageway led straight to the front door. Closed doors on both sides indicated other rooms. The nearest on Gallant's left as he inched his way silently forward was wide open. From that opening the glow of lamplight spilled weakly on to the floor of the passageway, lightly touching Gallant's dusty boots. He could smell alcohol, sweat, stale fried food. There was the faint impression of heat, too, and that heat came from a smoking oil lamp and from the barrels of the outlaws' rifles and six-guns, which every now and then banged deafeningly in dangerous defiance. The stink of cordite threatened to overwhelm the foetid aromas of men living rough. It stung the tender membranes of Gallant's damaged nose, caused him to blink away tears, for an instant to step back.

It was as well that he did.

No sooner had he withdrawn than he caught the murmur of conversation followed by the thud of boots. A long shadow fell across the floor of the passageway as one of the outlaws strode towards the door. He came out into the gloom, whistling through his teeth. From his hand a shiny six-gun hung loosely, smoke dribbling from its muzzle. The heavyset figure turned to slouch his way towards the back room. He caught sight of Gallant and jerked upright as if hit by a charging steer.

'My sincere apologies,' Gallant said softly. With shocking speed he whipped his six-gun up and around in an arc. The killing blow was aimed at the outlaw's head. It caught his left arm. Accustomed to knock-down, stomping brawls in sawdust saloons, the man had raised it instinctively to parry the blow. The sickening crack was of metal on bone. The man's eyes gleamed. Yellow teeth were exposed as a wild grin split his unshaven face. Still whistling thinly through his teeth, he brought the six-gun up to his right hip and reached across with his left hand to fan the hammer.

Gallant kicked the weapon out of his hand. It

clattered hard against the door jamb, thudded into the lamp-lit room.

Big fists clenched, the outlaw lowered his head and charged, swinging wildly. Gallant sidestepped and delivered a second powerful chopping blow with his six-gun. It connected with the nape of the man's neck and knocked him off his feet.

He lay face down, not moving.

His six-gun had come to rest on the floor just over the threshold. The shooting had stopped. The silence from within was ominous. Backed against the wall opposite the room, Gallant listened, waited. He calculated that there was but one man in the room. The fallen six-gun would have warned him of his companion's demise. He was sure to react. Gallant waited nonchalantly, keeping his own gun at the ready and his eyes on the pool of lamplight for the moving shadow that would betray the outlaw's intentions.

At his feet the fallen outlaw moaned, twitched, struggled to rise. Gallant smiled wickedly, and kicked him hard in the ribs. The man choked, subsided. He rolled on to his back. His black eyes raged at Gallant.

Inside the room, there was the whisper of stealthy movement. The pool of light in which the stunned outlaw lay rippled eerily across his prone body from feet to face. The man inside the room, Gallant surmised, had picked up the oil lamp. He was clever enough to realize his shadow would betray his intentions, and had moved the light.

But what was he up to? Gallant lacked a plan. He couldn't poke his head around the door without getting it shot off, and he couldn't see through walls.

He decided to wait him out.

Even as he made the decision, there was a sudden flurry of movement, a whirring sound. Trailing smoke, an oil lamp whirled out of the room in a high, looping arc and exploded against the passageway's opposite wall. Glass shattered, tinkled to the hard floor. There was a splutter, then a soft whoomp as the hot oil burst into flame. The man on the floor was engulfed. His shirt was alight. He screamed in terror. There was the stink of burning hair as he flapped at his head with both arms. Bucking and kicking, he rolled blindly, went the wrong way and splashed into the pool of blazing oil.

Gallant was already moving. He rammed his six-gun into its holster. Teeth gritted, he stepped into the flames. Heat seared his face as he bent to grab the man by his ankles. Common sense was screaming at him to drag the man along the passageway to the back room, and safety. Instead, a perverse primal instinct drove him the other way. He gripped the burning man's ankles with both hands. Vulnerable to attack from behind and unable to draw his six-gun, he heaved the outlaw's dead weight out of the lake of fire and stumbled backwards into the room lit by the flames now licking up the passageway's wooden walls.

The room was empty.

The window was a black, empty frame. Cold night air brushed Gallant's scorched skin like the caress of a cold hand. In the flickering yellow light he saw a table, scattered playing cards, bottles of hard liquor. But while Gallant was viewing the accommodation, at his feet the burning outlaw was dying in agony. What

Gallant needed was a cloth, a blanket, anything to smother the flames. In that bare room there was nothing.

Outside in the darkness there was a sudden shout, a burst of gunfire. Muzzle flashes lit the room, luridly outshining the flames. There was a howl of agony, another rattle of shots. Then silence.

Desperate, Gallant released the burning outlaw's ankles. He reached into the flames, grasped the man's burning shirt. It ripped. He thrust his hands under the man's arms, laced his fingers at his back. Grunting, he lifted the man's considerable weight. Bracing his legs, locking his arms, he made a fast half-turn and threw the outlaw bodily out of the window. He winced for him as the man's burnt clothing and skin raked bloodily across the jagged fragments of glass in the frame. The drop from the window ledge was about five feet. As the outlaw landed, Gallant heard a sharp crack. He grimaced, then without hesitation dived through the window.

McCrae was waiting for him. He was lit by the light of the rising moon and the glare of flames that were already poking their tongues through the roof and reaching for the dark trees.

'I shot the first one out of that room; you threw the second out on his head and conveniently broke his neck. Or should that be inconveniently? If those boys were the Brannigans, I think between us we've wiped out the clan.'

'Let's talk about it where it's cooler,' Gallant said, grasping his arm and pulling him away from the now furiously burning timber building that had been the

Travis homestead.

'We could try drawing water from the well, and dousing the flames,' McCrae said, straight-faced.

'Or use it to anoint two dead bodies and bring 'em miraculously back to life,' Gallant said drily. 'Come on, you fool, let's get out of here. We've wiped out at least half of an outlaw gang and burned down their house. Let's see what damage we can do to the town of Buck Creek.'

NINE

The moon was a bright orb floating high above Lone Cree Ridge when they collected their mounts and rode away from the blazing building. Dew had dampened grass and earth in the shadows under the high bluff. It kept the dust of their passing to a minimum. They rode at a good pace, on eager, rested horses. Gallant was sore from the flames; if he thought about it, he likened the feeling to that experienced by a soldier who has foolishly fallen asleep, without his shirt, in the heat of India's midday sun. But apart from that minor discomfort, he and McCrae had sustained no injuries, were untouched by knife or bullet.

'I killed the man we saw running from the privy,' Gallant said after a while, nudging his roan close to the journalist. 'Caught him cold inside the back door, and it was him or me. The man in the room, the man whose neck snapped when I threw him out the window, he drenched his own comrade in burning coal oil. Looked at that way, his death was retribution, so don't feel bad about it.'

McCrae flashed him a quick glance. 'I don't, not for

THE KILLING OF JERICHO SLADE

one minute. But what happened back there has dented my confidence. I'm left with the feeling that we stand no chance against men who would die rather than be taken.'

'With their boots on, or so folklore has it,' Gallant said.

'Incidentally, the men I saw, by the back door and the one who came out of the room, they didn't look Irish. What about that first man out?'

'Mexican.'

'Dammit. We raided the roost, and not one of the men there was a Brannigan.'

'Hardly surprising. Why hole up in a run-down ranch house when there's a saloon in the family?'

'Rooms above, girls down below and all the beer they can drink.' Gallant grinned in the moonlight. 'I can taste it, smell it, feel the cool glass already in my hand. But if I'm not mistaken I can see the town's lanterns flickering warmly through those trees ahead – and we're on the wrong side of the creek.'

'Buck Creek,' McCrae said, nodding, harness jingling as he took his horse off the trail and over the grass towards the glint of water. 'If we find them there, those Brannigans, and one of them killed that boy, we'll be up against it again. I don't think they'll give up without a fight.'

'For which,' Gallant said happily, 'all Irish boyos are renowned.'

It was long after midnight when they splashed through fast-flowing water and rode the short distance from grassy bank to trail and from there into the town of

Buck Creek. If such desolation could be so honoured, Gallant thought. What passed for a main street was wide, stony wasteland between scattered shacks. False fronts leaned drunkenly from rickety business premises, revealing sagging roofs of holed and rusting tin. Oil lamps hung from hooks high above the remains of rotting plank walks. Further away, dim lamplight glimmered through net curtains draped across the windows of hovels fronted by broken-wheeled, canted buckboards or top-buggies from beneath which cats, emerald-eyed in the moonlight, hungrily watched the two riders.

'Welcome to paradise,' Gallant said. He drew rein halfway across the wide expanse of packed and rutted dirt that passed for a street, and sat rubbing his chin.

Alongside him, McCrae grunted. 'You realize Melody's here?'

'By God, so she is,' Gallant said softly, saddle creaking as he rested both hands on the horn and looked around at the desolation. 'You and I, we were so busy drilling holes in desperadoes, that young lady got forgotten.' He smiled crookedly. 'Misremembered, as I've heard it put.'

'An Irish turn of phrase if ever I heard one,' McCrae said, 'and as it's the Irish we're after I'd say that building over there is where we should be heading.'

Gallant chuckled, but there was a chill in the sound that ruled out any suggestion of good humour.

'The Drop Inn,' he said, looking at the sagging sign. 'Unless it's been renamed the Shamrock. Open still at this late hour, if those dim lights and hitched horses are anything to go by. But ominously quiet.'

'At this time of night,' McCrae said, 'any men remaining at the bar will be hard put to stand, let alone talk.'

'I remember mentioning rooms above the saloon when talking about the Brannigans,' Gallant said, looking across at the building, its upper windows like dark holes punched in the sun-bleached timber wall. 'A look around suggests luxury hotels are bogged down in the planning stage, so—'

'For God's sake,' McCrae said.

He flicked the reins and set off for the saloon. Gallant grinned and tucked in behind him. It was a ride of about fifty yards. Closer inspection of the two horses at the saloon's hitch rail revealed them to be worn-out, sway-backed nags, which told Gallant that the men they were hunting – if they were here in Buck Creek – kept their horses safely stabled. But where, in such a godforsaken settlement? And where was Melody Lake?

Dismounted, their horses tied to the rail, both men stood for a moment looking at the saloon's warped timber door. Gallant, listening hard, heard the muffled murmur of voices. A clearer, more confident bellow of laughter. He looked at McCrae.

'We play this how?'

'Play it straight. You're after that little boy's killer. Say so – then wait for a reaction.'

'Is that the journalist's technique.'

'One of 'em,' McCrae said, and pushed in through the door.

Heat and the stale odours of beer and sweat hit

them in the face. The Drop Inn's interior was a surprise. The dim light came not from old, smoking tin lamps but from elaborate brass appliances. They were hung high from chains looped around rafters, their wicks turned down either for intimacy or to save oil. They threw yellow light on a bar that stretched the length of the long room. Two men as ragged as the ponies they had left outside stood drinking, hats on, hair straggling. Most of the tables filling the rest of the room were empty.

At the far end of the room, alongside a closed door, there was a dusty black piano. At its side a young woman with painted face and lips and wearing a bright scarlet frock stood leaning against the black wood, her elbow on the instrument's top. Two beer glasses stood there, half full. On the other side of the piano a tall man in a stained white Stetson stood with both arms folded on the top of the piano, watching her.

A thickset man sat on the piano stool. His fingers rested on the yellowing ivory keys. He glanced up at the young woman, grinned, and his hands moved across the keys. And as, haltingly but recognizably, the beautiful opening notes of the 'Londonderry Air' tinkled in the stillness, Gallant glanced quickly at McCrae, and nodded.

'By God, we've got company.'

The big man behind the bar spoke loudly, his voice carrying to every corner of the room. He'd watched them walk in dragging a pool of moonlight, slamming the misaligned door behind them hard enough to wedge it shut and bring down gritty dust. He was tall, with shoulders like an ox. His startlingly white apron appeared to be full length, tied with a belt under his paunch. His black hair, combed straight back, was glossy in the lamplight. Blue eyes were as watchful as those of a hovering hawk.

Gallant grinned as he reached the bar.

'Drinks all round, landlord,' he said, and the silver coins he slapped down jingled on the solid boards. 'Tell me, was that blasphemous greeting meant as a warning?'

'A warning, he says,' said the big man, and he looked around in mock amazement. 'Now who in the world would I be warning, and why?'

'Not these two sozzled beauties, that's for sure,' Gallant said, clapping the drunk nearest to him on the shoulder, knocking him off his precarious balance so that he stumbled against his equally drunk companion. 'As to why, I'd say it's because those two boyos who perked up at the sound of your voice had asked you to keep your eyes skinned.' He grinned. 'I notice the music's stopped. And after the overture, doesn't the play commence?'

'Boyos, he says now,' the big man said softly, and the amazement had gone from his gaze to be replaced by wary speculation. 'If for some reason they had done that, those *boyos*, I have to say that the arrival of your good selves would have caused me no alarm.' He moved away, splashed beer into glasses, stepped back to place them carelessly before Gallant and McCrae.

'Appearances,' Gallant said, drawing a finger through the beer splashed on the bar top, 'can be deceptive. Let me demonstrate. Your name's Brannigan. You're the new owner. The two boys over there talking to the young lady will be your sons.'

The big man stared. The speculation in his eyes had hardened to suspicion. 'I'm Eamon Brannigan, yes,' he said. 'But who the hell are you?'

'Born Gallant. Those words constitute a name, by the way, not the manner in which I left the womb. My colleague is Stick McCrae.' Gallant jerked a thumb. 'And those fellows down there, are they your sons?'

'For a stranger you ask a lot of questions,' Brannigan said, raising an eyebrow. 'But the English, now, they always were uppity, too damn sure of themselves.'

Gallant grinned. 'Guilty as charged. And history's warning me that I'm unlikely ever to be your close friend. But I'd still like an answer.'

'Why? And if the answer's yes, that they are my sons – what then?'

There was a veiled threat in the soft words. It was given added weight as, at the other end of the room, a chair scraped noisily across the dirt floor. Gallant flashed a glance to his right. The stocky man had risen from the piano and, with the man in the stained white hat, was heading towards the group at the bar. One was tall and ropey, the other short and bullish. Both were clad in rough range wear and wore six-guns on belts with loops in which shells shone brassily.

Behind them, the young, painted woman had straightened and stepped away from the piano. She seemed to be hesitating, standing watching the drama she knew was about to unfold, her face pale in the lamplight.

'What then?' Gallant said, echoing Brannigan, his pulse quickening.

'Why, we talk to them, that's what. We ask questions about a tragic accident they may have witnessed. A young boy died. Someone fired the gun. Someone *killed* that youngster, and so far they've got away with it.'

'It happened in Dodge City,' McCrae offered. 'My friend here's on a crusade. I'm a newspaperman. I came here to get your story.'

'If you want my story, it's not me you should be talking to,' Brannigan said mildly. 'It's Sean and Patrick who will tell the tale. Good Irish names, you will notice, and they are two fine boys who were instrumental in bringing their father across the sea and setting him up in business.'

Suddenly the two young men were upon them, crowding Gallant and McCrae, muscling close. There was no good humour in their dark eyes. They brought with them the smell of stale sweat and the raw reek of danger.

The sudden, electric tension communicated itself to the two drunks. On the outside of the group now, knocked sideways along the bar, they abruptly turned away, staggered towards the door on unsteady legs and stumbled away into the night.

'Good Irish names, yes,' Gallant agreed. 'As to *fine* boys, I'd say that's debatable. There's a rumour circulating in these parts. The suggestion is that the bundles of banknotes that brought you to America – and bought you this establishment – were acquired unlawfully. To be precise, carried from banks in gunny-sacks by men who authorized their withdrawals with levelled six-guns.'

'If it's a rumour you're repeating, Gallant,' the elder Brannigan said, both hands planted on the bar, his mild tones now edged with steel, 'I'll allow that you're an ignorant bastard and let it pass this once. But if it's an accusation you're making, you can be damn sure Sean will—'

He broke off as there was a sudden fierce bang, a scraping of boots. The tall man leaning hard into Gallant had grabbed him by his shirt front and slammed him back against the bar. His stained hat went flying, revealing bright-red hair. Teeth bared, he reached down, drew Gallant's six-gun and sent it skidding along the bar top. Eamon Brannigan slammed a hand on it, then pushed it so that it dropped behind the bar. At the same time the other brother, short and muscular but quick to react, plucked the six-gun from McCrae's holster and sent it clattering across the room.

'Sean will, and he has, and he'll do a damn sight more.' The man was leaning into Gallant, grinding the words from between clenched teeth. His forearm was up under Gallant's chin, forcing him back painfully against the timber bar's sharp edge.

'I admire your enthusiasm, but could you steady on, old chap?' Gallant said as pleasantly as he could manage. 'Use that throat for talking and eating, you know, rather fond of it and you're elbow's not doing it much good.'

The inane words were so unexpected they left Sean Brannigan nonplussed. Gallant saw the Irishman frown and his eyes dart from side to side as he tried to make sense of what he'd heard.

'D'you mind?' Gallant said politely, but this time the words were accompanied by a blur of action. One hand flicked up to grasp the Irishman's wrist with fingers of steel. Effortlessly, he eased the forearm away from his throat. Then, looking at his attacker with wide-eyed innocence, he brought his other hand hard up between the man's legs and imagined he was cracking walnuts by grinding them together.

Sean yowled. Both hands grabbed for his groin. His head dropped forward as he doubled up. On its way down his face met Gallant's elbow on its way up. Nose gushing blood, eyes streaming, suddenly the Irishman was bent forwards yet falling backwards. He hit the dirt floor on his backside, rolled on to his side and curled up, moaning.

Gallant's downing of Sean Brannigan had taken seconds. Behind the bar, Eamon Brannigan stood frozen. His other son, Patrick, had moved with the speed of youth and had McCrae in an armlock. The newspaperman's face was screwed up in agony. Any sudden movement of his upper body would leave him with a dislocated shoulder or a broken arm. Not caring for either prospect, he lifted his foot and brought his heel raking down Patrick's shin and instep.

Now it was the shorter Irishman's turn to howl in pain. He hopped on one leg. Purple with rage, he threw more muscle into the armlock. Viciously, face contorted, he yanked McCrae's arm higher. McCrae roared, tried again to find the Irishman's shin. Then

Patrick braced his shoulders and flung the newspaperman from him. McCrae hit a table, fell helplessly across it to the accompanying crackle of splintering wood, and collapsed on the floor amid the ruins.

Again, only seconds had passed.

Gallant was keeping his eye on Sean. He was still curled up and moaning, clutching his groin, but now one hand was at his holster. His fingers fumbled at the butt of his six-gun, slid off, and his curses turned the air blue as Gallant moved over to complete the job for him and tuck the Irishman's six-gun in his own holster.

Away to one side, Patrick was favouring his scraped leg, but moving grimly towards Gallant with big fists clenched. Worse, while watching both of the brothers Gallant could see out of the corner of his eye that big Eamon Brannigan was making a move. The saloon keeper, black eyes glittering with evil intent, dipped a hand beneath the bar as Gallant moved to stop him. He was too late. When the big man straightened, he was clutching a sawn-off shotgun.

Winking cheekily at him, Gallant coolly scooped up a full glass of beer and hurled it with the skill he'd honed playing cricket. Trailing liquid, it hit Brannigan between the eyes. The glass was thick. It hit bone with a crack. Even though it was a glancing blow, Gallant swore later that he could clearly see the cruel dent where Brannigan's nose had broken. Beer splashed into the saloon keeper's eyes. Blinded, blood leaking from both nostrils, he rocked backwards as the beer glass caromed off the top of the bar, bounced on the floor and rolled in the general direction of the door.

Then what felt like a tree landed on Gallant's back. It was Patrick, the brother who was all weight and muscle. He'd taken three running strides away from McCrae then hurled himself through the air. He wrapped his legs around Gallant's waist, one arm around his neck. Gallant grabbed at the splayed fingers that were clawing at his eyes, and fell sideways against the edge of the bar. He hit with the sound of a freight train slamming into wooden buffers. With his arms raised, his ribs were exposed. He felt one of them crack, winced as pain knifed clear down his leg. Then he was falling, sliding down the bar's rough front with splinters snagging his shirt and drawing blood from his face. He hit the dirt floor. Patrick rolled on top of him, placed an elbow in the nape of his neck. With a succession of solid blows he tried to separate the Englishman's head from his shoulders.

Close by, there was a crackle of wood. Gallant, the back of his neck being chopped with the bony point of an elbow and his face ground into the dirt, felt a spark of hope. He swung an elbow backwards – goddammit, two can play at that game – contacted hard muscle and when there was a pause in the relentless pummelling he forced his face to one side so he could breathe. Squinting through streaming eyes, he saw McCrae clawing his way out of the table's wreckage. The newspaperman made it, and rushed to join the fray. He launched himself at Patrick, stopped well short, and swung a vicious kick. The point of his boot took the Irishman behind the ear. His head banged against the side of the bar. He went limp. Suddenly the weight on Gallant was that of a man as good as dead. Gasping, every breath agony, he wriggled free, found Patrick's six-gun and tossed it to McCrae.

As he did so there was a tremendous double explosion that brought dust down from the rafters.

Sean, up on his feet, was stopped in his tracks. The dazzling flash of light turned night into day, lit every corner of the room. Then it was gone, leaving everyone with bright-red after-images and a ringing in the ears. But nothing could prevent them from hearing the bellowing voice of Eamon Brannigan.

The shotgun was held high. Smoke trickled from its twin muzzles. Brannigan had pulled both triggers.

'Fun and games, is it?' he roared. 'All right, then if yous want 'em, I'm your man – but, by God, if you play games with me it's a hard time you'll be having.'

While talking thickly, angrily, he was ramming cartridges into the shotgun. Poking them home with his thumb, he worked without looking. His furious gaze was directed at Sean and Patrick as well as Gallant and McCrae – and with greater intensity, Gallant realized; the man was directing his rage at his sons, and Gallant wondered if that suggested the big man knew of their lawless ways, had accepted them for what they had bought him but was now blaming them for bringing all sorts of trouble down on his head.

The shotgun snapped shut, clacking loud in the uneasy silence. Sean had slumped into a chair, his head in his hands. Patrick was a limp and bulky shape wedged in the angle between bar and floor. He was still out cold.

Gallant had quietly moved away from the bar. McCrae had instinctively positioned himself off to one side, ensuring that they offered Brannigan two well-separated targets.

But Brannigan had a shotgun. Was he likely to use it in cold blood? Certainly its threat had Gallant and McCrae hog-tied. By seizing that potent weapon Brannigan had left them nowhere to run, nowhere to hide. And the look on his face as he came out from behind the bar sent a chill down Gallant's spine.

'Never mind looking sideways at those two boys of mine,' Brannigan said, his voice menacing. 'One's down and out and the other's concerned about his manhood. Going by what's happened, I'm not at all sure it was there in the first place. Their stupidity brought you poking your nose in, yet when you walked through the door bold as brass they hadn't the brains or beef enough to handle you.'

'There was no need to try,' Gallant said. 'McCrae came to write about you, an Irishman who'd made good. I had questions to ask about a young lad's death. Your boys could only have considered that a threat if they had something to hide. By attacking us, they were as good as admitting guilt.'

'The guilt of bank robbery, but not of murdering a child.'

'The two are linked,' Gallant said. 'One of the men who robbed the bank in Dodge City put a bullet in that young lad's chest. But it was a stray bullet. It's possible the robbers didn't hear of the tragedy until days later. On the other hand—'

'Enough,' Brannigan snapped, and at the table Sean's head lifted as if he had detected purpose in his father's voice. 'They couldn't handle you, so it's down to me.'

'I could ask you those questions instead,' Gallant offered. 'They'll have confided in you. You'll have the answers.'

'It's too late for that. I'm putting an end to it.'

'For some reason,' Gallant said, 'the sound of that makes me go cold.'

Brannigan ignored him. His face, when he shot a look at McCrae, wore the look of a man facing unimaginable horrors. He waggled the shotgun at the newspaperman.

'Move over and join your friend.'

'I like it here.'

'Then that's where you'll die.'

The silence was numbing.

'Either my mind is playing tricks, or. . . .' Gallant frowned in disbelief. 'You want us standing together so you can cut us to shreds with that shotgun, feed the bloody scraps to your dogs?'

'One way or another, it's finished. If it'll make it easier you can hold hands while I do it. Turn your backs. Or if you want, I'll blindfold you with a couple of bandannas.'

'You're bluffing.'

'You think I want my boys hanged for murder?'

'Nothing's been proved.'

'They were there, in Dodge, I know that, at the very minute that young boy died. They could argue their innocence in a court of law, but that town marshal, Liam Dolan, he will push for a conviction to further his political ambitions.'

'The verdict's out of his hands.'

'Sure it is – but in the few short months that have passed since I left Ireland, I've learned a lot about Western justice, and not much of it inspires confidence. If a conviction seems doubtful, Dolan can always whip up a crowd, egg them on to a lynching.'

Gallant looked into the man's eyes, and saw nothing there but grim determination. He took a deep breath, looked across at McCrae and in the young newspaperman's eyes saw the same stubborn determination: McCrae would stand firm, hold his head high, not give an inch.

Playing for time, Gallant deliberately hesitated, then shuffled his feet and, shaking his head, walked slowly over to McCrae. The time he gained was minimal. And for the duration of those few short paces, try as he might, he could see no way out of their terrible predicament.

'I guess this is it,' he said, clapping the newspaperman on the shoulder. He stepped in close, met McCrae's eyes, saw a sudden light spark in their depths and knew McCrae believed he had come up with a plan. Gallant gave a bleak shake of the head.

But that was for Brannigan's benefit. He knew Brannigan was watching him, and though Gallant could see no way out he had not given up hope. While there was life. . . .

He could hear the saloon keeper's boots on the dirt floor as he came away from the bar. In his mind, while still facing McCrae, Gallant reminded himself of the relative positions of . . . well, the combatants. Sean at the table, feeling sorry for himself; Patrick lying against the bar, but now stirring, gasping and groaning as he struggled to rise. And big Eamon Brannigan.

Gallant swung around.

The saloon keeper had walked to within a few feet of Gallant and McCrae. He was caressing the shotgun. One hand grasped the worn pistol grip, the other slid up and down the gleaming barrels as if he were looking for some kind of justification in the warmth lingering there from the previous shots. Then he raised the weapon. Not high. Just enough to tuck the stock under his right arm. He clamped it there with his elbow. Right hand still grasping the pistol grip, he poked his finger into the trigger guard. His left hand was holding the forestock. He twisted his body, turning himself sideways so that the shotgun's twin muzzles swung towards Gallant and McCrae.

At the table, Sean Brannigan muttered, 'Holy mother of God,' and crossed himself.

'Cold-blooded murder,' Gallant said, feeling the hairs prickling at the nape of his neck.

'Only if there's witnesses who will talk,' Brannigan said.

'God's your witness, old chap – how d'you get around that?'

'By staying alive and out of His way,' Eamon Brannigan said, and his knuckle whitened as his finger tightened on the trigger.

The shot, when it came, was a taut crack.

Gallant blinked, felt his legs go weak. Behind him, McCrae grunted as if struck.

Sparks flew from the shotgun – but from the barrels themselves, not the muzzles. Along with those sparks were splinters of wood chipped from the forestock.

They flew like needles into the saloon keeper's face. As if by an invisible force the shotgun was plucked from his tight grip. It hit the floor, bounced and was then forgotten as a clear voice rang out from the other end of the room.

'If one bullet from my rifle can pluck the shotgun from a man's hands without harming a hair of his head,' the voice cried, 'all of you Irish fellows, think what I could do if I went for the man himself – and take that as a warning.'

Gallant took a deep breath.

'Well, knock me down with another of those feathers,' he said in a voice that held more than a trace of a tremor. 'I know I'm beginning to sound like one of those newfangled recording thingamabobs Edison's playing with, but I reckon that's the lovely Melody Lake yet again – and she's turned up in the nick of time.'

TEN

'Not sure it becomes you,' Gallant said, reaching out tenderly to touch Melody's cheek. 'Overdone the red paint on the lips, and that frock is the wrong colour for your complexion – if we could see it through that ghastly face powder, which we can't. And what on earth is a dance-hall girl doing strutting about with a Winchester repeater?'

'You're babbling,' McCrae said.

'Tend to do that when I'm scared witless,' Gallant said.

'Well, scared or not,' Melody said, 'we have to do something about these three boyos.'

Gallant chuckled. 'Don't think the patriarch of the family likes that term.'

'But boyos they are,' Melody said, 'every one of them, and if you want to find out more about what went on in Dodge on that fateful day, get talking to them before they build up another head of steam.'

Eamon Brannigan had retired behind the bar. The shotgun rested on the timber counter. The saloon keeper was staring broodingly into a shot glass of whiskey, while using a grubby rag to dab at the blood speckling his glistening face. Probably railing mentally at his own stupidity, Gallant decided, as much as at Melody's audacious marksmanship.

Sean had joined his father, and was leaning close, talking quietly but urgently to him. Clearly recovered from Gallant's mistreatment of his private parts, there was now an ugly look in his dark eyes. His first move when he walked behind the bar had been to pick up Gallant's six-gun. He was simmering, dangerous, armed with a handgun and too close to the shotgun for Gallant's comfort.

Patrick was unarmed – McCrae still had his pistol – but was recovering fast. He was a bull of a young man. His recovery from the knockout had been impressive, and now he was pacing restlessly up and down, glancing from Sean and his father to the little group consisting of Gallant, McCrae, and the astonishing Melody Lake.

Waiting for a signal from his pa, Gallant deduced. But if it comes – what then?

'When in doubt,' Melody said, watching him, 'take the bull by the horns.'

Gallant grinned. 'Weren't you supposed to be doing that: interviewing Eamon Brannigan for the newspaper?'

'Well, when I rode in I thought the town looked like hell on earth. I was pretty certain you two would wind up here, and end up needing help—'

'Doesn't do much for my self-esteem,' McCrae protested.

'—so instead of brandishing my notebook and

100

pencil, I applied for a job.' She grinned, pouted with red lips and swished the skirts of the scarlet frock with a twitch of her slim hips.

'Said help was most gratefully received,' Gallant said soberly, 'and now I'll take your advice.' He glanced at the newspaperman. 'Back me up, Stick, into the lion's den and all that rot.'

Carefully avoiding the glowering, stalking Patrick, Gallant crossed to the bar. He leaned on it close to where Brannigan and Sean were talking. Both men looked up and glared. Sean's fists clenched. The saloon keeper's hand slid towards the shotgun.

'Leave it,' Gallant said. He smoothly drew the six-gun he'd taken from Sean and placed it on the bar, cocked.

'That scattergun's not been reloaded,' Gallant pointed out, 'and killing us didn't quite work out so why don't we call a truce? Landlord, you can serve the drinks. If you had a peace pipe on a hook somewhere we could pass it round the circle, puffing reverently – but never mind, I'll settle for your best moonshine whiskey.'

Brannigan sucked his teeth angrily, looked sideways at his son then reached for glasses and a bottle. Liquid splashed, and as McCrae joined them at the bar all four men raised their glasses and tossed back the fiery liquor.

Gallant sucked in a breath to cool his burning throat. When he was able to, he said, 'Sean, when your daddy was set on squeezing that shotgun's trigger and ending a young Englishman's life, he let slip that you and Patrick were in Dodge when the kid, Jericho Slade, died.'

'We were in Dodge. The Slade boy died. If you're trying to make a connection, there isn't one.'

'I'm not even going to ask what you were doing there. For all I know, you could have been taking flowers to your sweet, white-haired old grandma. All I want from you is your version of what happened. To put it bluntly, did you see the kid die?'

'The way I heard, there was some shooting and he took a stray bullet over by the general store.' Sean shook his head emphatically. 'From where we were, we couldn't *possibly* have seen him.'

'And you would have been on the side of Front Street closest to the bank, at a guess,' Gallant said thoughtfully, wondering what Sean meant and knowing the bank robbers would have had a clear view across Front Street. 'You said "we". Who was that, exactly? I take it Patrick was with you. But who else?'

'A couple of hardcases: Jensen and Malone. Another, a Mex, Lopez, stayed back at the Travis spread.'

Gallant nodded, grimacing at distasteful memories. 'I think we've met all three of them, in circumstances that did them no good at all.'

Sean's head jerked up. He frowned.

'In case you're worried, they didn't have much to say,' Gallant said, and McCrae turned away, smothering a grin. 'As for who was there in Dodge City, Sean, haven't you missed someone?'

'You mean Billie Flint? Hell, he's just a kid. From time to time we let him hold the horses while we did the hard work. On that day we told him we were riding into Dodge, and he tagged along.'

'Why don't you tell us what this is really all about?' Eamon Brannigan said, staring at Gallant. His hand was shaking when he poured himself another stiff drink. He knocked it back, coughed, and said, 'You've been asking your fine questions, Gallant, but never really getting to the point – am I not right? So get down to it, man. You know they were robbing the bank there in Dodge. Ask them if they were involved in gunplay. Ask them if it could have been one of their bullets that killed that young boy. And when that's done, and settled in their favour, then you can tell me why you're here on this goddamn crusade when it's well known that it was young Billie Flint that let loose with a big gun he'd never handled before in his life; young Billie Flint that is to hang for that killing.'

'Billie Flint's dead,' Gallant said, 'shot down in the woods by the posse that went after him when he escaped the hangman.' He touched his skinned cheek, waiting for a response to the news. Then, recognizing that they hadn't heard of his involvement, he went on, 'But Billie Flint was wrongly accused. He didn't kill that little lad. Even Liam Dolan admits he was wrong. So who did? Jensen, or Malone? Or was it one of your boys, Brannigan? According to Sean, that's impossible, because they couldn't see the youngster. And what I want to know is: why not? The general store's right across the street from the bank. They *must* have seen him.'

'Wrong, because at the time we're talking about, that store there was just about finished taking in supplies,' Sean said. 'A freight wagon was standing in the street. Muleskinner waving his whip, getting set to move off. We couldn't see the kid because we couldn't see any part of the damn store.'

'A *freighter* was there?' Gallant said, and suddenly his memory lurched backwards and he was once again arriving in Dodge City and handing a gold double eagle to a big man dressed in rags who spat tobacco through a stained black beard.

'If you're familiar with that cattle town,' he said, 'you would perhaps have seen that freighter more than once? Drunk your fill next to the big muleskinner in the one of the town's many saloons? Exchanged pleasantries?'

'I didn't say he was big,' Sean said.

'Most of them are.'

'Yeah, well, you're right. I drank with him from time to time, and I can tell you that not many come as big as Sebastian Bullock.'

'Bullock,' Gallant breathed, and he shook his head at the sheer beauty of coincidence. 'But if you couldn't see the store because dear old Sebastian's wagon was in the way—'

'That lets us out, doesn't it?' Sean cut in, grinning, now openly mocking Gallant. 'If we couldn't see the store from across Front Street, then the bullet that killed Jericho Slade must have come from someplace else.'

PART THREE

ELEVEN

The air in the Dodge City jail's office was hazy with cigarette smoke. Marshal Liam Dolan was the culprit. He was leaning back in his swivel chair, tilted Stetson almost hiding his eyes. His booted feet were up on the oak desk, alongside a dented tin cup that held the gritty dregs of cold coffee. A smouldering cigarette drooped from his lips. White ash discoloured the front of his denim shirt, and a heap of mashed cigarette ends overflowed the brass ashtray and spilled on to the paper-strewn desk.

It was long after midnight, and he'd been sitting smoking one cigarette after another for more than an hour. He was a worried man; worried about his future; wondering if he had one.

All had seemed rosy. He'd worked his way into the good books of Morton J. Slade, a respected senator. Then Slade had seen his son die in the town where

Dolan was the chief law officer. The young man destined to hang for that brutal killing, Billie Flint, had escaped the gallows, then died at the hands of the posse hunting him down. Dolan had been the man in charge of that posse. So far he had managed to keep the details of how that young man had died under wraps.

The marshal reached up with his hand and wearily knuckled his bleary eyes. Then he tilted his hat back, and raised his eyes as if appealing to heaven for salvation.

Billie Flint's father was also a politician. So, in one way or another – though never directly, he liked to think – Dolan was responsible for the deaths of two politicians' sons. And all this was at a time when Morton J. Slade had been seriously considering Dolan for a top security position on his Washington team. Dolan had been dreaming of an office in the White House; of putting his feet up on a desk bigger and shiner than his scarred, Dodge City monstrosity.

Those dreams seemed to have gone up in a puff of smoke, he thought bitterly – and he sucked on his latest cigarette, then flicked it viciously at a tin wastebasket.

The door banged open. Keno Lancing walked in. The burly deputy, Dolan noted, still bore the marks of his encounter with the enigmatic Born Gallant. It was a fight the deputy was not likely to forget; he had vowed to get even with the Englishman, if their paths should cross again.

Each lawman had been brooding over his own particular troubles. And Dolan's troubles were also

Lancing's, for the marshal had promised to take the deputy with him if he made it to the nation's capital.

Always observant, Dolan brightened a little when he noticed that Lancing was looking like the cat that's purred its way into a feline heaven and found it rich in thick cream. So he waited; tilted back his chair; yawned in studied indifference.

'The boys just rode into town,' Lancing said. 'Left the buckboard with Franklin Land. He lent them a horse and saddles to see them back here.'

He walked around the desk, shook the coffee pot, heard liquid sloshing and clattered it on to the hot stove.

'So Billie Flint's made it back home,' Dolan said. 'What was his pa's reaction?'

Lancing shrugged, flicked the coffee pot with a fingernail, reached up to a shelf for a tin cup.

'You don't know,' Dolan said, 'or you don't care?'

'What I care about is what's useful to me.' Lancing reached across the desk for Dolan's makings. He dropped into a chair and began fashioning a cigarette.

It had gone so quiet in the room that the rustle as the grains of tobacco sprinkled on the paper was clearly audible. Lancing smiled, squinted across at Dolan. 'What I'm saying is that what's useful to me is useful to both of us, and our high and mighty ambitions. So you'll be pleased to know that when the boys were bringing the empty buckboard away from Guthrie Flint's, they spotted Stick McCrae doing his best to stay out of sight in the woods.'

'McCrae?' Dolan was frowning. 'The woman, Lake, was heading down to Buck Creek to talk to Eamon

107

Brannigan. But they work for the same paper, so what was McCrae doing there? And how does that help us?'

'Whatever he was doing, he had company.'

Lancing licked the paper, sealed the cigarette, put it between his lips. Deliberately avoiding the marshal's increasingly frustrated gaze, he found a match, scraped it on his boot sole, lit the cigarette. He blew a stream of smoke, followed it with his eyes as it added to the haze.

'Christ,' Dolan said, 'are you going to tell me, or keep it to yourself?'

'McCrae was there with the Englishman, Born Gallant. When they thought the buckboard was safely out of sight, they rode down to Flint's house.'

'And from the look on your face when you walked in, you think that's good news.'

'I think it has possibilities,' Lancing said, crossing to the stove with the cigarette drooping from his lips, and splashing scalding hot coffee into his cup. He reached for Dolan's, refilled it, put it on the desk by the marshal. Then he sat down again, cocked an eyebrow at Dolan and waited.

'Gallant's after Jericho Slade's killer,' Dolan mused, sipping the hot coffee, thinking aloud. 'Billie Flint didn't do it, so Gallant'll figure it has to be one of the other bank robbers. Guthrie Flint and his boy didn't see eye to eye, but they were close. So Flint must have talked to the boy. I'd say he knows about the Travis spread, knows the Brannigans hole up there with Jensen, Malone and Lopez. Somehow Gallant worked that out. He figured a visit to Flint would provide him with that information.'

Suddenly he grinned at Lancing.

'And now you see what I'm getting at,' Lancing said.

'Storming the Travis spread when the pack's at home would need a small army. Two men?' Dolan shook his head. 'No, it can't be done.'

'That's what I mean about possibilities,' Lancing said. 'The Englishman's brash, too big for his boots. He thinks he can take those boys; him and McCrae. With luck, this could be the end of both of 'em.'

'Maybe,' Dolan said, frowning again, 'and maybe not. Lately, the only luck coming our way has been bad.'

'So somehow two men overpower five, is that what you mean? And maybe it goes beyond the Travis spread; they have to go to Buck Creek to finish the job.' Lancing shrugged. 'It could happen, sure. So let's say it does, Gallant and McCrae get lucky. All right. Nothing changes, because the way I see it, their luck becomes our luck. What overpowering those five leads to is Gallant finding out what we've known all along.' He paused, let the suspense build. 'Jericho Slade,' he said softly, 'wasn't killed by the bank robbers.'

Dolan's face was a shade grimmer. But again he was nodding, because he was following the deputy's train of thought, and liking what he saw.

'If Gallant knows that, it won't take him long to work out what it means. When he has that understanding, the only course open to him is to head back here, to Dodge.'

'To do that,' Lancing said, 'there's only one route he'll take if he's in a hurry.'

'Which leads to more good news. There's bad weather brewing. It's never easy spreading blankets with the wind flapping them like sails, then trying to sleep under dripping trees. But short of making the ride in one spell, he and McCrae'll be forced to stop.' Dolan grinned. 'Now, if they stopped at the Flint place on the way out, befriended the man, wouldn't it make sense to try the same again?'

He leaned forward, badge shining in the lamplight, and stretched out his arm. Lancing did the same. The two men clinked coffee mugs in a toast. And in the warm fug of that jail office, there was an evil glint in Liam Dolan's eyes as he expressed his immense relief in a low, chilling laugh.

TWELVE

It had begun to rain. Driven by a strong wind, the rain came out of the darkness in blinding, ice-cold sheets that drenched the three riders and forced them off the trail into a stand of trees. Their exposed skin was slick, their hair plastered to their heads, their teeth chattering. For some bodily warmth they dismounted and huddled close together in a circle formed by the three horses. The water they drank from canteens taken from saddlebags was lukewarm; the bottles went some way to warming their hands. Then, with no other options open to them, they donned slickers to cover clothing already soaked through and resumed their ride with gritted teeth.

Buck Creek was already an hour away down their back trail. Before the rains came they had skirted Lone Cree Ridge and seen in the near distance away to the east the faint glow in the trees that was all that remained of the Travis spread.

Gallant was feeling somewhat dazed, and he knew that Stick McCrae must be in a similar state. What had started with polite conversation in the elegance of

Guthrie Flint's house had led to gunfire and the death of Jensen, Malone and Lopez at the house that was now a heap of glowing embers. That bloody battle had been followed by a violent physical confrontation with the three Brannigans at the Drop Inn.

Thanks to the inspiration that had led Melody Lake to gain temporary employment as a dance-hall girl – clothing provided – and once again make use of her skill with a rifle, the confrontation had left both sides battered, bruised, but alive. But for Gallant it had done much more: it had, as far as he could tell, solved the puzzle of Jericho Slade's death.

Hence their hurried departure: Marshal Liam Dolan had some explaining to do.

'We had two choices at the start of this ride,' Gallant called now, his voice buffeted by the wind. 'Push on to Dodge in one go, pacing the horses, or stop halfway for a few hours' sleep. This confounded weather has changed everything. We've got to stop, so what do you say to bedding down in the woods for what's left of the night?'

'What I say,' McCrae retorted, 'would be unprintable.'

'But would change nothing.'

'Another idea,' McCrae said. 'If we get close enough to the embers of the Travis spread we'll be warm and dry, snug as bugs.'

Gallant heard a tinkling laugh, and marvelled yet again at Melody Lake's resilience, and spirit.

'I never did believe in retracing my steps,' she called, 'and the Travis spread is back a ways. Guthrie Flint's place, on the other hand, is by now just a short way ahead of us.'

'Dammit, she's right again, you know,' Gallant said, dashing rainwater from his face with the back of his hand. 'Melody, my sweet, did you know it was Guthrie Flint who told us all about the Brannigans and their uncouth crew? That's what sent us to the Travis spread and Buck Creek.'

'And, as I recall,' McCrae said, 'one of his parting shots suggested he was dismissive of our chances of ever leaving the Travis spread alive.'

'That settles it, then,' Gallant said. 'Tally-ho, you two. Guthrie Flint deserves to learn how we got on, and for telling him the inspiring story of our exploits, painted with vivid colour, you can be sure we'll get a bed for the night.'

Straw was tickling Gallant's neck. Dust was irritating his nostrils. Stick McCrae's snoring – very much akin to the snorting of an angry bull – was adding to what counted as mild torment, and Gallant had been lying half-awake for a good hour.

But he was a happy man. Another noise he was listening to was the sound of the wind and rain battering the timber walls of the loft. There was also a steady dripping coming from somewhere in the loft's darkness, but Gallant was listening to that and the storm's ceaseless battering with great contentment for, thanks to Guthrie Flint, he was inside, not outside. Thanks to the councillor, their horses had been cared for – from time to time he could hear them moving in stalls almost directly below and Gallant, McCrac and Melody Lake had been served a delicious, late dinner.

They were well fed, safe from whatever the elements could throw at them and had left the Brannigans nursing their wounds back in Buck Creek. For the first time since he had ridden along Front Street into Dodge City and broken up a neck-tie party, Gallant could rest easy. With that comforting thought in mind, that's exactly what he did. And as he slipped into sleep he realized that Stick McCrae had stopped snoring and, at long last, the storm was easing.

How long he slept he did not know, but he was woken by a different noise, and it was a noise that brought him rolling out of his blankets and fumbling in the darkness for his holster and Sean Brannigan's six-gun.

As he did so, a hand touched his shoulder. Stick McCrae was already awake.

'Riders came in from the Dodge trail,' he said in a low voice. 'Rode up to the house, hammered on the door. That woke me. Guthrie must have had a lamp lit. I could see the yellow light through the chinks between the boards. Then I heard them talking. Two men and Guthrie, voices low, then raised. Sounded as if Guthrie was arguing, but getting nowhere.'

'The two men – anyone you know?'

'Liam Dolan and his deputy, Keno Lancing.'

'Glory be,' Gallant said quietly, 'they've come all this way and saved us a long ride.'

McCrae snorted. 'The exact opposite. From what I could make out, they're intent on taking you on that long ride, and if I'm any judge it will be your last.'

'Is that so?' Gallant said. He smiled grimly in the darkness, listening to the voices drifting across the

114

yard, the scraping of boots; sensing growing impatience and a heightening of tension. 'Guthrie seems to be standing firm, but he's a tired man, outnumbered, and they represent the law.'

McCrae was close to the wall, his ear to a crack.

'It's done, over.' A door slammed. 'That was Guthrie, departing; he's gone in.'

'Having told them where we are, and washed his hands.' Gallant squinted across at McCrae, seeing his face as a pale blob in the gloom. 'I never was my usual sparkling self in the hours before dawn, but even befuddled by sleep I can work out what this means.'

'They're accusing you of murdering Guthrie Flint's son, Billie,' McCrae said, and he came away from the wall, his boots rustling through the dry straw. 'Gallant, if we're going to stand a chance of getting out of this we'd better wake Melody—'

'No.' Gallant reached out, grasped McCrae's arm. 'When we bedded down she found herself a nest behind some hay bales. If she stays there—'

'Here they come.'

'Dammit, I can hear them, man, and there's no way out of this place other than through those big doors down there.'

'Then that's where we face them – and God help us.'

There was the whisper of steel on leather as McCrae drew his six-gun. He was halfway to the black square that was the loft's hatch before Gallant moved, was descending the shaky ladder with awkward haste as booted feet splashed across the yard.

Gallant dropped off the ladder and joined McCrae

in the mustiness of the barn. The lawmen had borrowed the oil lamp from Guthrie. Through the wide doors Gallant could see the reflected light from the lamp wavering in the pools of storm water as the two men approached. That sixth sense all animals have was causing their horses to stomp nervously in their stalls. There was a soft whinny that told eloquently of their uneasiness.

Me and you both, Gallant thought, and he whispered, 'We take the sides,' and he pushed McCrae to the left. Then he drew his own six-gun. With one eye on the doors, the inky wetness of the night and the shifting lamplight, he began moving to his right.

The gloom, and haste, were his undoing. A wooden rake was lying half-covered in straw. He trod on the tines. The shaft rose out of the darkness and hit him in the face. Pain knifed through his nose. Shocked, cursing himself for a fool, he stumbled backwards, tripped, and fell flat. He flung his arms sideways. His knuckles hit the hard floor, his fingers opened and the six-gun rattled away to be lost.

Then Dolan and Lancing were running into the barn. The light from the lamp spun wildly, lighting the timber walls, the ladder, the straw-strewn floor where Gallant was desperately rolling, seeking cover. Then there was a crash, the tinkling of glass and the light went out.

Instantly, it was replaced by vivid flashes that turned night into day as Dolan and Lancing opened fire.

Dirt spurted in Gallant's eyes. A second bullet punched a hole in the wall close to his face as he threw himself behind a pile of old saddles. As he did so he saw flashes from across the barn as McCrae returned fire. With no fire coming from Gallant's direction, it was as if the two lawmen instinctively sensed his help-lessness. They ignored him, turned away from his position and concentrated their fire on McCrae. Fierce volleys forced the newspaperman back against the wall, drove him to dive for cover that did not exist.

Gallant felt sick.

'All right, that's enough, Dolan, stop firing,' he called, shouting over the din. 'Stick, it's over, put down your gun.'

The firing stopped. In a space reeking of cordite, the silence was like a leaden weight, depriving a man of spirit.

'You saying it's over is not enough,' Liam Dolan called, turning towards Gallant. 'It's over when I give the word – and I'll do that when you walk out of there with your hands high, Gallant, and ride with me to Dodge City to face trial for murder.'

'Wouldn't dream of missing it,' Gallant said. 'Always happy to see a cocky lawman make a fool of himself in a packed courtroom.'

As Gallant stepped over the saddles and moved forward with his hands high, he saw the glint of white teeth in the gloom as the marshal grinned.

'Don't bank on that happening,' he said. 'And, McCrae, I want you with us. You're a newspaperman. I want you along to see everything's done according to the law.'

The two lawmen stood back, guns at the ready. Dolan jerked his head, silently ordering them to get on with it. Gallant and McCrae walked deeper into the

117

barn, opened the stalls and collected their horses. They took time saddling, then mounted and rode towards the big doors. As Gallant glanced across at McCrae he knew that the same thought had entered both their minds: a break now might be the only chance they'd get. Then, for some reason, the idea dissipated like smoke. They rode past the marshal and his deputy, out into the rain. It was slashing across the yard again in icy sheets, as if paying them for their stupidity.

Gallant felt numb. He knew damn well that when Dolan said he wanted everything done according to the law, his words carried a hollow ring. It was the ring not of truth, but of deceit laced with triumph.

Up in the loft, Melody Lake heard everything. The explosion of noise had brought her bursting from her snug corner with her Winchester already cocked. Hesitating, quelling her desire to spring into action, she had listened to the talk, the gunfire, the ultimatums, and had heard Gallant and McCrae ride out of the barn into the storm.

A few minutes later, now standing by the hatchway listening intently, she heard the four men ride off, up the slope in the direction of the stand of trees from where Gallant and McCrae had watched deputies driving away an empty buckboard. She stayed where she was, listening to their hoofbeats fading in the distance. Then a frown furrowed her brow.

A staccato clatter of hoofs came from behind the house. A single rider rode off at speed. And for the first time since she was dragged unceremoniously

from a deep, peaceful sleep, Melody Lake was puzzled.
What the hell was going on?

THIRTEEN

'There was nothing I could do,' Guthrie Flint said. 'If I had carried on arguing they would have searched the barn anyway. In politics I'm a reasonably important man, but that wouldn't have stopped them arresting me for obstructing justice. So I told them just enough. They were, after all, expecting to find only Gallant and McCrae. I assumed that for privacy you would be sleeping well away from the men. If so then they would do their damnedest to keep you out of it, and there was no reason for me to mention your name.'

Melody Lake was standing in Guthrie's kitchen. The councillor had come to his front door and, unable to see her, had called her name. He had quickly heated the coffee pot as she came down from the loft and splashed across the muddy yard, had poured two drinks and watched with some amusement as she tugged off her filthy boots inside the front door. In the kitchen Melody took the hot cup with muttered thanks, but her mind was still on the sound of that single rider pushing his horse hard in the direction of Dodge City.

Flint was a towering figure wearing a fancy silk dressing gown of a rich shade of purple. He was leaning back, his ample hips against an oak cabinet. Melody was pacing, the coffee cup in one hand, in the other her Winchester repeating rifle. Her glance kept drifting towards the window, the darkness outside. After a moment she muttered something unladylike, then swung to stare at Flint.

'You know what's going to happen, don't you?'

'Dolan is taking Gallant to stand trial.' He waited a moment. 'I think there's a possibility that may not happen.'

'A possibility?' Melody laughed drily. 'Gallant and McCrae will never reach Dodge City. They'll die trying to escape,' she said bluntly. 'Haven't you heard of that old ruse? Conveniently for Dolan, Gallant's guilt will die with him – although I'm sure you know he had nothing to do with your son's death.'

'If you heard me arguing with those officers,' Guthrie said, 'then you'll know damn well what I think.'

'I heard,' Melody said, nodding her satisfaction. 'I also heard a rider leaving in a hurry. Who was that?'

'I have a man who works for me. This is not a ranch, but there are stables and he looks after those, sees to the horses, the grounds.'

'It's not yet dawn. There's a storm blowing. Where's he going at this time?'

'Dodge City.'

'Really?' Melody lifted an eyebrow, her mind racing. 'The way he was pushing that horse, and assuming he knows a way to avoid running into them, he'll be there before Dolan and Lancing.' Deliberately, as if it would be tempting fate, she made no mention of Gallant or McCrae.

Guthrie was smiling his understanding. 'That was exactly why I sent him out so soon after they left, with instructions to make haste: I want him in Dodge in plenty of time to apprise Senator Morton J. Slade of the situation.'

'Slade's there?'

'He will be.'

'And what's this situation?'

'The message the rider will relay is that a man called Born Gallant has almost certainly discovered the identity of his son's killer. He is to tell the senator that it would be to his advantage to await that man's arrival.'

'Because the killer will be unmasked?' Melody's face was grave. 'But what if Gallant doesn't get there? That'd really spoil your plan, wouldn't it? Put you in old Morton's bad books.'

'I'm confident Gallant will make it.'

'Why?'

'For two reasons. The first is that he is a most unusual man, with extraordinary talents; he has a way of putting people off their guard.'

'That's as maybe. But he and McCrae are unarmed. They're being held captive by two men who, somewhere along that trail, will shoot them dead.'

For several moments there was an uncomfortable silence, both of them deep in thought. Melody had put down her empty cup and was agitatedly twisting the rifle. Her mind was a long way down the trail, her ears filled with the sound of gunshots and the squeal of frightened horses, her imagination painting vivid pictures of horror.

A wave of nausea washed over her. She turned to Guthrie, despair in her eyes.

'I should have killed them where they stood—'

'No.' He was shaking his head. 'That would have been a mistake.'

'Who for? Me? You think I'd care about that? I'd've saved two young men from cold-blooded killers hiding behind a badge.'

'And become one yourself.'

'I told you, I don't care.'

'Listen to me, my dear.' Guthrie paused, waited for her breathing to settle, for the wild light of panic to leave her eyes. When she'd calmed down, he went on.

'I said there were two reasons why Gallant will make it to Dodge City. The first is that he is an unusual man, and could perhaps make it on his own. But I believe the second reason makes his success nigh on certain. He has a hole card. It was up there, hidden in the loft above my barn.'

Melody was wide-eyed. 'I take it you mean me. So first you don't want me to shoot Dolan, now you do – is that it? Ride out there, gun him down? If it is, what's the difference between dropping him and his partner in the barn, and out there on the trail?'

'That's not what I'm suggesting. Gallant and McCrae must know that Dolan and Lancing will use their guns to ensure they don't reach Dodge. Somewhere along that trail, they'll risk everything and try to make a run for it – won't they?'

'Damn right they will. But if they do, I won't be

there. My horse is not the best, and it's worn out.'

'There's a thoroughbred in my stables. Strong, fresh, raring to go.'

'With that,' Melody said, sudden hope bringing colour to her cheeks, 'I could overtake them easily. But that would be the easy bit, and then—'

'I've heard you are a resourceful young woman, Melody Lake,' Guthrie said. 'So listen carefully, my dear, because this is what I want you to do.'

FOURTEEN

'They shot Billie Flint in the woods to the east of Dodge,' Gallant said. 'I've got a feeling Dolan enjoyed that, would like a repeat. Thrash us up through the wet undergrowth, quick bullet in the back, that sort of thing.'

'If he does,' McCrae said, 'we haven't got long to live.'

'True, and that's bad news. Sis is running the place back home because the only male offspring's playing silly beggars somewhere in America. That's yours truly. If I die, the good name of the Gallant dynasty dies with me. Can't let that happen.'

'You got a plan?'

Gallant grinned. 'Planning's not my strong suit, old chap. Tend to await events, then react with deadly effect.'

They rode for a while in silence. The storm was dying, but not without a fight. Heavy black clouds were scudding across the bright face of the moon, trailing behind them long skirts of icy rain driven by a blustery wind. Through it all the four men had been riding at a pace that covered a lot of ground. Dolan and Lancing had positioned themselves some thirty yards behind their prisoners, and maintained that distance over terrain that was uneven, and slick with mud. They were ideally placed to cover any sudden break by Gallant and McCrae.

'I'm all for going now,' McCrae said after a while. He'd turned in the saddle, glanced back at the two following lawmen, seen the shine of their slickers, the vapour from the horses.

'Beats taking it lying down,' Gallant agreed. 'There's some cover now; trees, scrub. If we split, go off the trail on either side, we could be away and out of sight before they know what's happened.'

'You for it? They're talking now. Hear them? First time they've done that, so it could be decision time. If it is, and we wait, it could be too late.'

'Last chance, then,' Gallant said. 'Let's take it. Move when I give the word.'

He took a deep breath. Looked again at the wet tangle of growth under the trees on either side of the trail, the deep shadows, braced himself for the coming swift break, the inevitable hail of bullets. With the murmur of the lawmen's voices in his ears, Gallant chose his moment and opened his mouth to give the snapped command—

He stopped short. Somewhere behind them a rattling volley of shots rang out. It was followed by the drum of hoofs, rapidly growing louder.

Gallant hauled on the reins, turned his horse, squinted back into the darkness. Alongside him McCrae's horse was stepping backwards as the newspaperman tried to hold it still to see what was happening. Some thirty yards back, Dolan and Lancing had also pulled up and turned their horses. Gallant's immediate thought was that they were off guard. If he and McCrae were going to get away, there was surely no better time. Even as his pulse quickened at the thought, their chances were increased as a bank of cloud raced across the moon and sheets of blinding rain swept out of the darkness.

But with the rain came an apparition. The sleek horse was black, its coat a glistening wet sheen. On its back the rider was a slim form wrapped in a cloak of black cloth. Horse and rider were moving like the wind and might have raced by in the blackness, continued without pause into the night, leaving nothing behind but the fading clatter of their passing. Instead, with a spray of wet mud and a scraping of hoofs on the underlying hard stone, the rider hauled on taut reins and dragged the horse to a sliding halt. Even as it turned, tossing its head, snorting, rearing, a shrill scream set the hairs on Gallant's neck prickling. It was a scream of panic, a woman desperately appealing for help.

'Oh please, please, someone,' she cried, 'he's being attacked, his life is in danger, you must help him!' Almost completely shrouded by the cloak's hood, her face was a patch of white framed by strands of wet dark hair.

'Who, where?' Dolan yelled.

'A ways back down the trail. It's Senator Slade, he is on his way to Dodge City and—'

'What's that you say, *Morton J. Slade's* being attacked?'

127

'Yes, yes, a gun has been held to his head and lawless men are demanding his money, his gold rings, oh please, hurry, do something.'

Dolan swung on Lancing, his eyes alight.

'Stay with these two. Hold 'em, you hear me? I'll go back, do my damnedest to save his bacon.'

'And rescue our ambitions,' Lancing said, flashing a savage grin in the darkness.

Dolan swung his horse. Its hoofs kicked up water as it pranced lightly around to face back down the trail.

'You going to show me the way, guide me to the senator?' he called across to the woman.

'Oh no, no, I'm exhausted, distraught, but you surely won't miss him, he is with a small group and they are all being held. . . .'

To one side McCrae, listening intently, was shaking his head.

'Dear God,' he said softly, 'isn't she amazing?'

'If that's who I think it is,' Gallant said, 'Lancing's got trouble.'

Branches clattered overhead as the strong wind gusted, spraying droplets as Liam Dolan flicked the reins and raked his mount's flanks cruelly with his spurs. 'Hold them,' he called again over his shoulder as the horse leaped forward. Then he was gone, racing away to be lost as the trail dipped and curved in the darkness.

'Damn, I suppose that means we wait here in the rain while he plays the knight in shining armour?' Gallant said loudly to Lancing.

While talking he was slow-walking his horse to one side of the trail, putting the deputy between him and the woman. Lancing was forced to watch him, thus turning his back to the cloaked rider. McCrae, recognizing the subtlety of the manoeuvre, did the same, but made it appear as if he was merely giving his horse free rein.

'We should push on to Dodge,' the newspaperman said.

'That was never the intention,' Lancing said.

'Well, blow me,' Gallant said, and he shook his head in wonder. 'I guess I owe you a dollar, Stick.'

'Guess you do, though as I've won the bet it follows that I'll never get to spend it.'

Lancing was listening to the talk, watching the two men carefully, his eyes wary. He suspected a trick. A thin smile cracked his lips. Moving smoothly despite the cold and the wet, he drew his Colt.

'Dolan said to hold us,' Gallant said. He frowned. 'You going to finish it here and now?'

'We'll wait,' Lancing said. 'Move off the trail into the woods. There's shelter there from the wind and rain.'

'Which all sounds very pleasant,' McCrae said, 'but we could be there for a very long time if Dolan decides to stay with the senator.'

From behind Lancing there was a light, lilting laugh.

'That's very unlikely, Stick, because you surely know there is no senator,' Melody Lake said. Her words were punctuated by a metallic click. 'Throw down your gun, Mr Deputy. If you make one wrong move, you're a dead man.'

Gallant saw Lancing's eyes narrow. He'd recognized

the click for what it was, and the muscles in his jaw bunched as he realized his danger: his back was presenting a broad target to a young woman holding a gun no more than ten feet away. He had recognized the voice now the fake panic had been dropped, had seen her many times around Dodge City. The reputation that had followed her to the cow town, the tales of her exploits in Salvation Creek, he had always regarded with scepticism, even outright disbelief.

Suddenly, Lancing's world had been turned upside down.

His eyes burning with fury, he lifted his hand, opened his fingers and let his six-gun splash into the mud. Then he turned in the saddle and looked at the young woman. In one hand she held the Colt revolver with which, a mile down the trail, she had fired the shots that had attracted Dolan's attention and led to his undoing. With the other she now swept back the cloak's hood. Shaking loose her wet hair, she smiled at Lancing. All the while the pistol remained rock steady, and her dark eyes were dancing even as the rain, lighter now, splashed her pale, upturned face.

'Oh, how the mighty have fallen,' Gallant remarked, and he saw a tremor shake the deputy as the truth finally hit home. 'Tricked by a slip of a young woman. And all down to hubris, right? Dolan's arrogance, his desperation – and you damn fool enough to hang on to his coat tails.'

'If you think this marks an end to it, you're wrong,' Lancing growled through clenched teeth. 'It's a long way from over.'

'Oh no, it will be over very soon,' Melody said. 'I

have it from Guthrie Flint that Morton J. Slade really is on his way to Dodge. The senator wants his son's killer convicted and hanged. I think Born Gallant will bring him good news.'

'So now you've got rid of your gun,' Gallant said, 'you'd best trot along after your boss. When you find him he'll be riding round in circles and feeling humiliated, so your first task will be to wipe away his tears. After that, you can give him the good news: when the two of you ride into Dodge City – provided you've got the guts – the whole town will know the name of the man who killed Jericho Slade.'

FIFTEEN

The rain had ceased; the dying wind was an old man's breath creaking though the tall trees. Deputy Keno Lancing, leaving his pistol submerged in the sloppy mud, cast a baleful glance at the watchers then turned to canter with surly reluctance down the trail in search of the marshal.

'He'll find Dolan, and they'll be back,' Gallant said. 'When that happens, we need to be miles away.'

The pistol Melody had used to effect the trick and disarm Lancing had been lent to her by Guthrie Flint. She handed it over to Gallant, who slipped it gratefully into his holster. McCrae turned down the offer of the Winchester, telling Melody with a wry grin that if it came to trouble he'd rather she was protecting him than the other way about.

Then, with a final glance down the saturated trail, cut up by so much recent use, they turned their horses towards Dodge City and set off at a measured pace that would cover a lot of ground in a hurry while not pushing their mounts to exhaustion and beyond.

Out in the open the torrential rain had turned the

prairie into a vast plain of sodden grass. Great clods of earth were thrown up by the horses' pounding hoofs. As one, the three riders spread out, and rode in line abreast. Melody Lake, shaking her head and dashing wet filth from her face and eyes, settled in the middle. Gallant flashed a grin at her, and she stuck out her tongue. Her cloak was wrapped around her, the hood up. She rode with one hand on the reins, the other holding the wet cloth tight against her throat. That garment, too, had been handed to her by Guthrie Flint. The councillor's plan had been carefully thought out, and it had worked a treat.

Nevertheless, victory in one small skirmish didn't mean the war was won. Gallant believing he knew the name of Jericho Slade's killer wasn't enough. To get the man convicted – to get him through the doors of a law court as an accused man – required rock-solid proof. Where, Gallant wondered, was that to be found?

It was Melody who drew their attention to the big freight wagon.

They had left another wooded section of the trail and, in the chill, pre-dawn light, found themselves on the wider east-west route that extended for many miles in either direction, linking the old cow towns.

It was Gallant who, as they overtook the lumbering transporter, recognized both the wagon and its black-bearded muleskinner.

'Sebastian Bullock,' he said, 'as I live and breathe. A stroke of pure luck. That man could settle everything and cook Dolan's goose.'

'Colourful language,' McCrae remarked.

'For a colourful character,' Gallant said. He pulled his horse away from his companions and, avoiding the big, iron-bound wheels and the fine spray of water, rode alongside the wagon.

'Remember me?' he called. 'I'm the chap who contributed a gold double eagle to the improvement of your wardrobe. I see you haven't acquired new trousers. What did you do, blow the money on strong drink?'

The response was a stream of brown liquid that was ejected from the depths of the beard and passed close enough to make Gallant sweat.

'Or perhaps it was tobacco,' he said, feigning mopping his brow.

Bullock's black eyes gleamed down at him with amusement. 'What are you up to now? Is it another hanging you're hoping for?'

'Ah. Nothing wrong with your memory, I see. Which is good, because I'm hoping you can help me solve a tricky problem.'

'If it involves mules, I'm your man. If it's more technical—'

He broke off and looked across in surprise as Gallant hooked an arm around a convenient bit of wood projecting from the slow-moving freighter, pulled himself out of the saddle and joined the mule-skinner on his seat. His horse trotted away. McCrae jogged across and leant down to pick up the trailing reins.

'A little boy was shot dead in Dodge,' Gallant said to Bullock, who sat enveloped in the stink of working mules and the big, sweating muleskinner. 'A little bird told me you were there. Your freighter was alongside the general store and you'd just finished unloading when all hell was let loose, hot lead flying, men ducking for cover. Tell me what you remember.'

Gallant pulled out a silver coin, twisted it slowly and contemplatively so that it glinted invitingly in the morning light.

'You can put your money, away because what you've said is as much as I know,' Bullock said, squinting sideways at the coin, then idly flicking his whip over his team's backs. 'Men came running out of the bank, waving shooting irons. There was a lot of wild shots, and one of them dropped the boy.' He spat his disgust.

'How d'you know?'

'Word came out of the marshal's office, spread like a fire through dry grass. A wild shot, it was said, but according to Dolan someone saw what happened, shouted across to him as he ran up the street.'

'Don't suppose this convenient witness was given a name? So he could be questioned by an impartial lawyer or town bigwig when the excitement had died down?'

'Meaning anyone except Dolan?' Bullock shook his head. 'Him and Lancing moved fast. They caught one of those owlhoots and locked him in a cell. Said he was the one killed the boy.' He twisted to grin slyly at Gallant. 'Would have hanged him, too, 'cept they didn't get the chance.'

'And a damn good job they didn't,' Gallant said, 'because you can take it from me it was no bank robber who shot that boy. He was on the plank walk by

135

the store, probably close to his mother. Your wagon was hiding him from the robbers' line of sight.'

Bullock pondered. 'Ah, but it could have been a robber, even so,' he said. 'If one of 'em was further up the street, and some way across, he would have seen around the wagon.'

'None of them were. They were outside the bank, stayed on that side of the street, then rode off in haste.' Gallant let that sink in, then said, 'There were two sides doing some shooting. The good and the bad. We know where the bad boys were. What about the good? Where were they?'

'Liam Dolan?' Bullock said, eyebrow raised. 'The town marshal, he came out of the jail. He saw what was going on up at the bank, came a-running. Pulled his gun—'

'And opened fire?'

'That he did.'

'And coming up the street he was well placed,' Gallant said carefully, 'to see the bank and the general store. If he could see the store, he could see the boy.'

'He had a clear view of him,' Bullock said, frowning. 'And now you mention it, he had me worried, Dolan did. Bullets were flying. There was a ricochet. I saw sparks, flattened myself against the wagon to save my life, heard the scream of the stray bullet.'

'But thought no more of it?'

'Later, yes. At the end of that day I saw the scar on my wheel. Not on the metal rim; on the iron hub.'

'But you didn't put two and two together?'

'I told you, yes, of course I did. I thought at once of the ricochet, knew that was what had happened.'

'But why didn't you think of the dead boy? You heard the ricochet, you knew the boy was dead—'

'I told you. The word was out that the bank robbers had killed him.'

'And what do you think now?'

'He was firing wild, Dolan. Caught up in the excitement. Maybe keen to get the job done fast and impress that senator, who was in town.'

Bullock turned and spat, away from Gallant this time. Then, more slowly, thinking it through, he said, 'And if what you've told me is correct, well now, it seems to me he was the only man in a position from where it was possible to kill the boy.'

With a flick of his thumb, Gallant sent the silver dollar spinning in the air. It was caught deftly by Bullock, and pocketed.

'Being given a bank robbery to foil must have seemed like a ticket to the White House for Dolan,' Gallant said, preparing to drop from the wagon. 'Instead, one of his wild bullets ended a young boy's life. If the truth were to get out, Washington would be a dream gone sour, his career as a lawman in tatters. With your permission, I'll use your name to make that happen.'

SIXTEEN

'How do we play this?' Lancing said.

'Nice and easy,' Dolan said. 'All cards are on the table. They think they have the pot, but they're wrong, the game's ours to win.'

'Gallant,' Lancing pointed out, 'will ride into Dodge and straight away go talk to the senator.'

Dolan snorted derisively. 'Talk's cheap. Accusations need to be backed up by solid evidence. Gallant rode to Buck Creek and listened to the drunken ranting of outlaws who were in Dodge City to rob the bank – and he believed what they told him. Nobody else will. Men of that kind lie habitually to save their own skins. Gallant has nothing that would stand up in court.'

Lancing had found the marshal after a couple of miles' hard riding, and together they had moved off the trail and ridden through wet, crackling under-growth under dripping trees. Now, in a small clearing, they were sitting on moss-covered logs dragged close to a crackling fire that sent shadows flickering across their faces, accentuating their sombre mood.

'You may be right,' Lancing said, flicking a cigarette

end into the fire's red embers, 'but we don't know how the senator will react to Gallant's news. We left young Barnard in charge of the jail. I can see the senator ordering the lad to raise a posse and station armed men around the town's perimeter. Right now the badges we're wearing are just so much tin. Morton J. Slade is a higher authority. We cannot risk riding openly into town.'

For a few minutes there was a lull in the talk. The stillness of the night was broken only by the sound of steady dripping from the surrounding trees; by the rasp of a match as Lancing lit another cigarette, the soft settling of a log in the fire that sent sparks shooting skywards like startled fireflies.

'Supposing Gallant does go and talk to the senator,' Dolan said at last, emerging from a period of deep thought. 'First he'll be confronted by an aide. Gallant will tell that feller the news he has is for the senator's ears only, and so the big man will see him in private.' He cocked an eyebrow at Lancing. 'You see where this is leading? Take away the messenger,' he said, 'and we're down to hearsay evidence. It's Slade's word against the word of the man Gallant names as his son's killer.'

The deputy looked at Dolan through a cloud of cigarette smoke. He nodded, his eyes speculative.

'So we make it into Dodge tonight, under cover of darkness. We find Gallant, and we shut his mouth for good.' Lancing studied the glowing tip of his cigarette, and frowned. 'The trouble is, there's not one messenger, there's three. What do we do about McCrae and the woman? And then there's Guthrie

Flint. How much does he know—?'

He broke off, looking up and staring, because Dolan was shaking his head.

'What Flint knows will have been reported to him by Gallant. With Gallant gone, we're back to hearsay evidence.'

'And the other two?'

'Don't let them worry you.' Dolan grinned. 'They're troublemakers; we get rid of them the way a horse gets rid of troublesome flies. With Gallant out of the way, Slade with a name but no proof, I'm back in charge. If McCrae or Lake start shooting their mouths off, their only view of sunlight will be through the strap-steel bars of a cell.'

He climbed to his feet, kicked wet earth on to the fire and stepped back as the embers hissed and spat.

'One other thing,' he said, watching the white vapour rise towards the trees. 'All the cards are on the table, and the game may be there to be won – but I take no chances. When we ride into Dodge, we split up. I'll go after Gallant. If I'm not man enough to handle a brash Englishman, I'm in the wrong job.'

'And me?' Lancing was frowning. 'What will I be doing?'

'You will be making damn sure that, in the unlikely event Gallant sneaks up behind me or gets in a lucky shot, we have a hole card that outranks all others and guarantees success.'

When they walked towards their horses, Keno Lancing, always quick to catch on, was grinning and shaking his head at Liam Dolan's devilish cunning.

SEVENTEEN

It was dawn when Gallant and McCrae rode abreast alongside the railroad tracks dividing Dodge City's Front Street. The town was not yet awake; the street was empty but for a horseman knuckling his eyes as he rode in and a gnarled teamster standing smoking a corncob pipe alongside his empty wagon. Behind them in the east the cloudless skies were streaked with brilliant light. Their shadows skittered ahead of them over the rutted street as if overjoyed to be home.

Or perhaps it was the improvement in the weather that was doing it, Gallant thought and, bridle jingling as he twisted in the saddle to peer back at the rising sun, he flashed a grin across at McCrae.

'Melody had the right idea, turning off and going home to bed. You do the same. I'll get a room at the hotel.'

'If you pick the best, Slade might be there.'

'I don't want to be that close to him. I want you to do the talking. As a newspaperman that comes easy to you.'

'This has been about you from the moment you

141

rode in and disrupted a hanging. I'm playing a minor role – observer, if you like. You should have the honour of talking to the senator.'

Gallant grimaced. 'It's an honour if I've got it right. What Sebastian Bullock saw suggests I have, but if I'm wrong, I'll be leaving town in a hurry.'

'Go book your room. I'll ride across to the jail and talk to whoever's been left in charge. They'll know where the senator's staying. I'll meet you' – McCrae looked up at the lightening sky – 'in an hour, at the café across the way.'

They parted on that note. Bearing in mind what McCrae had said, Gallant hitched his horse outside the smallest hotel he could find, roused the bleary-eyed owner, took the key from her and climbed the stairs to a room that was sparsely furnished, but clean.

An hour later he was sitting opposite McCrae and tucking in to a heaped plate of fried beef and onions topped by two eggs with golden yolks. Neither man said anything until the meal was finished, and they were sitting back with steaming cups of black coffee.

'Slade's staying at the house of a friend, a local town official,' McCrae began. 'He and his wife took the boy Jericho to Kansas City, where he was buried. Mrs Slade then went on by train to Washington. But Slade's hollow-eyed with grief, and cannot settle. There's a few clear days before he's needed back in government. He's spending them here in Dodge, desperate to see the killer pay for his crime.'

Gallant shrugged. 'To learn anything at all he'll be relying on Dolan. Dolan's not here. If he was, he'd be looking the senator in the eye while lying through his teeth to keep his job prospects alive and save his own neck. But Dolan will be back, you can be sure of that. We have to stop him before he can get to Slade.'

'Dolan's left a young deputy in charge,' McCrae said. 'A kid called Barnard, looks as if he should be sucking a pencil behind a desk in school, not single-handedly upholding the law in a town like Dodge. Dolan told him nothing, not where he was going, or when he'd be back. So, according to the deputy, the senator's pacing his friend's gallery and getting angrier by the minute.'

Gallant sipped his coffee, looked at the steamed-up window and through it the hazy street bright with morning sunshine, and smiled.

'They'll come in under cover of darkness,' he said with absolute certainty. 'Around midnight, I'd guess, when the town's sleeping. They'll ride in, leave their horses, then hunt me down on foot.'

McCrae nodded agreement. 'You're the driving force that's leading to his downfall, and he knows it. With you out of the way, he's in the clear.'

Again Gallant looked towards the window. 'They'll be expecting trouble. Any ordinary night, I'd be asleep in a hotel room. But Dolan's no fool, and after the confrontation with Lancing he knows I'll be waiting for them to show up.'

'Two of them, two of us,' McCrae said. 'Acceptable odds. And the advantage lies with us because we'll be waiting for them; they'll be riding into the unknown.'

But Gallant was barely listening.

'It would be a mistake for me to stay in town,' he mused. 'If I do that I have to be out and about, in streets mostly in darkness. I'm a stranger here. Dolan knows every street, every back alley, every run-down property.'

'In those circumstances, yes, that would give him the edge.'

'So I'll do the opposite to what he expects. Unless he and Lancing ride in a wide loop, they're going to come into Dodge from the east. When they do that I'll be out there, waiting.'

'I notice there's a lot of emphasis on what you will be doing,' McCrae said, watching him closely. 'If you're out there on the trail with a six-gun loaded with shells labelled Dolan and Lancing, where will I be?'

'Dolan got the job of Dodge town marshal, and held it,' Gallant said. 'He then caught the eye of a visiting senator, who must have seen something worthwhile in the man or he wouldn't have offered him a position on his staff. I think Dolan's good at what he does. If he's that good, he'll cover every eventuality. So you're going to be out there near that cottage tucked away in the aspens outside town. You'll be making sure Deputy Lancing doesn't get close to the lovely Melody Lake.'

Suddenly, Stick McCrae was grinning. 'Then you'd better tell her what you've got planned, and prepare for the storm,' he said as the cowbell hanging above the door clanked mournfully. 'Here comes that young lady – and by the look in her eyes, she's on the warpath.'

EIGHTEEN

Pushed by strong winds, the rain had moved far away to the west. Now the wind's strength had lessened. The merest whisper of a cool breeze stirred the leaves, and the land was covered by a motionless blanket of black cloud. The moon was struggling to break through but the night remained unusually dark. Gallant, under trees flanking the trail and sitting relaxed in the saddle alongside Stick McCrae, knew that they couldn't have wished for more favourable conditions.

'I felt sure you would argue with Melody,' McCrae said.

'She's a clever young woman. "You two head out of town," she said, "in case those two lawmen stay together. And in case they don't, I'll stay behind in the cottage and wait for Lancing." I knew at once it was the best thing she could do to stay safe. She'll be armed and ready in her own home. She's a crack shot with a rifle. If she's inside, he won't get near the house.'

'She'd have been safer somewhere in town, among people,' McCrae grumbled. 'She could have booked a hotel room, or bedded down in the office.'

'You may be right, but that wasn't in the options she gave us, Stick. There were just two: in her house, waiting for Lancing, or out here with us.'

'Yeah, well,' McCrae began – and then he broke off and lifted a hand in warning.

'Listen.'

'I hear them,' Gallant said, and there was a soft snick as he drew his six-gun. 'Horses. More than one, moving fast. But if there's two of them, then I was wrong about Lancing going after Melody.'

'Not two,' McCrae said, and now he was backing his horse. 'Into the woods, Gallant. They're closing fast. Can you see them? The sky's lighter on the ridge, they're outlined—'

'Four,' Gallant said. 'Four riders. Now what in the world does that mean?'

While talking he was swinging his horse and easing it sideways into the cover of the pines, his eyes always on the faint outlines of the approaching riders. He melted into darkness, on to a carpet of needles that muffled the sound of their horses' hoofs; into a silence that fell like a blanket over straining ears.

Then the riders were upon them, four men riding two abreast down the trail. On that black night there was little to distinguish them: dark clothing made darker by the heavy cloud cover, hats pulled low, the only brightness a highlight picked out on bridle metal, on a holstered revolver.

But one of the riders, as if sensing the presence of the men hiding under the trees, lifted his head and looked in their direction. For an instant his pale face

146

was visible, the glint of what little light there was caught in his searching eyes.

Then he turned away. The four horsemen moved on at the same steady, relentless pace, the sound of their passing fading as they headed for Dodge City.

'Well, I'll be damned,' Gallant said. 'Those two riders behind Dolan and Lancing were the Brannigan brothers. When Lancing found him, Dolan must have decided the day would be well spent in a ride to Buck Creek. And if he was able to do that because he's been pally with those Irish bank robbers for some considerable time, then suddenly there's an explanation for everything that happened in Dodge on that terrible day.'

NINETEEN

From afar, lit by a bright moon that had at last been set free as the cloud cover floated serenely westwards, Dodge City was a jumble of wooden packing cases split by the glint of iron rails laid to carry the rolling stock of the Atchison, Topeka and Santa Fe Railroad. Closer, Gallant and McCrae began to pick out details here and there: Chalk Beeson's Long Branch saloon; Fred Zimmerman's gun shop; the place midway where Gallant had destroyed the gallows. And as they drew closer still, entered the town limits and rode by the mouths of dark alleys that here and there separated those business premises, they were uncomfortably aware that any one of the four men they had followed along the trail could now be waiting in ambush.

Their mounts were taking them into town at a slow walk. Both horses had their ears pricked and were obviously nervous. And although that could be taken as a warning it was impossible to know what they could hear, and foolish to try to second-guess them.

'The bank robbery was staged by Dolan, with the

help of his Irish countrymen, to enhance his reputation,' Gallant said quietly, his eyes everywhere. 'There was meant to be a lot of shouting, a lot of shooting, ending with foiled bank robbers being driven out of town by Dodge City's upstanding marshal, Liam Dolan. But it went badly wrong. This time Dolan has to get it right, or he's finished.'

'Getting it right by shooting you down won't give the senator his son's killer.'

'It'll leave Dolan free to make up a plausible story. If he goes back to naming Billie Flint, with Flint and me dead who's going to argue?'

'Then with four armed men here ahead of us and intent on ending your life,' McCrae said, 'what are we doing riding boldly down the middle of Front Street like two men leading an Independence Day parade?'

'I'd like to think I lead a charmed life,' Gallant said, grinning. 'Truth is, this is the only part of town I know.'

Even as he spoke an errant cloud floated across the moon, plunging the street into darkness. Before their eyes could adjust, they were dazzled by a series of bright muzzle flashes from the closest alley. Gunfire crackled. It was followed by a succession of solid thumps as bullets hit living flesh. There was a snort as breath was painfully expelled, and suddenly Gallant was pitching forward as his roan's heart stopped beating and it went down. Gallant landed on his hands, rolled in the dust, his shoulder jarring in a deep rut. He was aware that McCrae was also down; the gunmen had gone for the horses to put both riders afoot.

The street was still in darkness, and Gallant took a moment to raise his eyes and give thanks to the drifting black cloud. Shifting his gaze to the north side of the street, he saw no sign of movement and guessed the sudden lack of light had also taken the gunmen by surprise. They had been waiting, looking over their sights at targets drawing ever closer and exposed in bright moonlight. Forced to open fire in a hurry when the light went, they had gone for the horses. That, Gallant thought, left him and McCrae alive to fight on, but they were not out of the woods. Front Street was unusually wide. No matter which direction they chose, to reach the safety of buildings they would have to cross thirty or forty yards of open ground.

All those thoughts raced through his mind as he crawled towards the downed horses. They'd fallen close to each other. McCrae was already lying prone behind his mount. Gallant wriggled close, put his horse's body between him and the alley and rolled on to his side.

'Two rifles,' he said. 'Probably Dolan and Lancing, but that's just a guess. Doesn't matter. It means the other two are waiting and watching elsewhere. That makes getting out of here a lottery. Which way do we run?'

'I can't tell you,' McCrae said. 'Knowing the town doesn't help. If we're going to take the fight to Dolan, we have to get close. If that means running straight at those guns . . . well, what does your army experience suggest?'

'Beat a tactical retreat,' Gallant said, and he chuckled. 'That's an army term for running away with our tails between our legs. But if we do that, the battle's lost. So, the alternative is to take the enemy by surprise. They'll be expecting us to take off across the rails to the other side of the street. If we do the opposite, it should buy us some time.' He squinted at the newspaperman. 'What did you call it?'

'Running straight at those guns.'

'Then let's do it, while the moon's still acting coy.'

Both men drew their six-guns. Gallant again looked up at the sky. The cloud was moving away slowly, but it was perilously close to drifting clear of the moon. A quick glance along the street to the east told him just how close it was, how little time they had left: bright moonlight spilling over the edge of the cloud was rolling towards them like an unstoppable flood.

'Damn it, let's go,' Gallant swore, and he climbed to his feet and leaped over the fallen horse. 'If we make it across,' he hissed, 'go to the right of the alley and up on to the walk.'

They ran hard and fast, as soundlessly as they could, separated by several yards to lessen the risk. Neither man fired his weapon. In the darkness it would take a few moments for the gunmen to realize the danger. Those seconds were precious. They covered half the distance without any reaction. Then they were spotted, and the rifles opened up again. At once, Gallant and McCrae changed from a straight, bee-line run to a zig-zagging, jigging approach that transformed them into flickering shadows in a pool of darkness. Bullets whistled yards wide. Gallant heard the gunmen calling to each other. Ahead of him the black shapes looming high against the night skies became recognizable as the false fronts of business premises lining the street.

Then the flood of moonlight was upon them.

They had ten yards to go.

From the shadow of the alley, someone laughed in triumph. A figure stepped out into the light. It was Sean Brannigan. He braced his legs, raised his rifle, took a bead on the fast-running McCrae.

Gallant pulled his six-gun, shot on the run and hit him in the chest. The Irishman was knocked backwards, his eyes wide with shock. The rifle fell from his hand. Then Gallant was up on the plank walk. McCrae was ahead of him, running away from the alley and close to the walls of a wine merchant's offices. Panting, they made it to the next alley separating the buildings, leaped from the plank walk and into the welcoming shadows.

'Dammit,' McCrae gasped, 'but that was close.'

'Too close,' said Liam Dolan out of the darkness. 'Hoist your hands, both of you, you're—'

Gallant spun, sprang out of the alley. A shot blasted as he leaped on to the plank walk. The bullet clipped the wall, brushed his sleeve, painted his arm with liquid fire. He flattened himself against the wall close to a window where frocks hung on display. With steady hands he poked the wasted shell from his six-gun, reloaded. Then he thought fast.

McCrae hadn't made it. Dolan couldn't reach Gallant without putting himself in danger, and he had to keep watch on McCrae. With McCrae a prisoner and out of action, Gallant had to rely on his own quick wits, his vast experience—

Then his head jerked up as, from the alley, another shot rang out.

Gallant closed his eyes, leaned his head back against the wall. McCrae, he thought grimly. *That bastard Dolan's shot him to shut his mouth for keeps. Melody, my dear, you stay where you are because this is no place for a lady.*

He opened his eyes again. A deadly calm swept over him. The muscles in his jaw bunched. Gallant looked to his right, across the alley. He caught a glimpse of stealthy movement. Patrick Brannigan had left his dead brother and was sidling along the wine merchant's wall. In the shadows his eyes caught the light of the moon. They were as green as a cat's. There was a steely shine from the six gun in his big fist. Then Gallant's skin prickled. Coming from somewhere behind him he heard the hard scrape of boots on wood.

It had to be Lancing. He was on the plank walk, and advancing boldly.

Then Liam Dolan stepped out of the alley.

'For Christ's sake shoot the dog,' the marshal roared. 'Down him now and put us all in the clear.'

But by stepping out of the alley he had blocked Patrick Brannigan's approach, forcing him to hold his fire. Lancing was coming in from the opposite direction. If the deputy obeyed the shouted order and missed Gallant, his bullet could kill Dolan.

Frozen in indecision, for no more than several fleeting seconds all three men hesitated.

In that brief hiatus, Gallant acted. He turned, crouched, then launched himself in through the draper's window. Wood splintered, glass showered and he found himself tangled in frocks of cotton and silk and ribbons of all the colours of the rainbow. Tearing himself free he hit the flimsy back of the window display area, fell through it and came up on his feet. He was in the main shop. Moonlight pouring in through the shattered window and wrecked garment display showed him a counter, more frocks on racks, fancy bonnets, men's broadcloth suits – and a door leading to the shop's rear.

Shots rang out behind him. Bullets smashed a case displaying cheap jewellery. It exploded in a glittering shower. There was a solid thump as the gunman came in from the plank walk. Gallant launched himself at the rear door at a run, kicked it open. He went through into darkness, blundered across a space littered with boxes, found another door let into the side wall of the premises.

There, Gallant slowed. Against the light, he could see the shape of the man following him: Patrick Brannigan. A bank robber and no stranger to violence, he was proceeding cautiously. To slow him further, Gallant snapped a couple of shots in his direction and was rewarded with a strangled curse, a thud as the outlaw tripped and fell.

Gallant tried the door. It was unlocked. He pulled it towards him, winced at the creak of hinges, stepped out into the alley and pulled the door shut.

Darkness. And a body, ominously still. McCrae, and he was as dead as a doornail, Gallant thought bitterly. He looked at the newspaperman's limp form. He had fallen on his side, and was facing Gallant. The pistol with which he had tried to defend himself was by his outstretched right hand. His eyes were closed. Around his head there was a pool of dark blood. Gallant looked away, swept by compassion and a genuine feeling of loss.

Then a noise behind him in the shop jolted him sharply back to reality, and his own critical situation. McCrae was finished. He, Born Gallant, English blue-blood, was on his own in a stinking alleyway in an alien land, hunted by two armed men and the noise that had startled him meant one of those men was creeping up behind him.

He eased himself away from the door. As yet unde-tected, he forced himself to relax and observe.

To his left, at the street end of the alley and bathed in moonlight, Dolan and Lancing were standing talking animatedly. Dolan gestured in one direction, Lancing pointed up the alley. Gallant smiled grimly. Intent on saving their own skins, they had sent Brannigan in after him. They must have heard the shots, but obviously they didn't know the layout of the draper's shop. Lord knew what Dolan had been indi-cating, but Lancing had clearly suggested to the marshal that there was bound to be a back door, and that that was the route Gallant would take.

What they hadn't thought of was a door let into the side of the building, and now Gallant was beginning to enjoy himself.

'I'm behind you, boys,' he called loudly, and flat-tened himself against the wall.

Both men spun round like startled deer. A fierce volley split the night's silence as they at once opened up with their Colts. But they might as well have been shooting at the moon. They could not see Gallant, who was in deep shadow, whereas they were silhouetted starkly against the light. As if realizing the danger, they ceased firing and began to move towards the cover of the buildings.

Telling himself not to rush, Gallant steadied himself against the wall. Then he took careful aim, fired a single shot and dropped Keno Lancing in mid-stride. The deputy fell. His head hit the edge of the jagged edge of the plank walk and he flopped sideways and lay with the stillness of death.

'Damned cold-blooded, unsporting and all that,' Gallant called to Dolan, 'but all's fair in love, war and a shoot-out in Dodge – wouldn't you say, old boy?'

Then the draper's side door opened and a dazed Patrick Brannigan burst out of the store, from darkness into darkness. Disorientated, he lurched away from the door in a stumbling run. Halfway across the alleyway he tripped over discarded crates, swore, regained his balance. When he looked down towards the street he saw Lancing's body up against the plank walk on the right. On the left, a man was disappearing around the corner of the draper's shop.

Brannigan jumped to the wrong conclusion.

He snapped two quick shots at the indistinct, fast-moving figure he took to be the fleeing Gallant. Splinters flew from the wall close to the man's head. Then he'd gone, out of sight. A grin split Brannigan's unshaven face. He chuckled hoarsely, shook his shoulders and pushed out his chest, and began to walk towards the street.

156

Gallant stepped out of the shadows, and rammed his pistol into the Irishman's back.

'I'd stick to robbing banks if I were you,' he said, 'because you're not cut out for this rough—'

Brannigan spun, swept the gun away from his back with his left hand and, with his pistol, chopped at Gallant's head. Gallant half blocked the blow with his forearm. Steel cracked against bone. Backing away from a second swinging blow that caught him on the back of the head and set his senses swimming, he tripped and went down. His pistol flew from his hand. Red lights flaring behind his eyes; he flopped on to the filthy ground, landed alongside Stick McCrae – and found himself looking into the newspaperman's open eyes.

McCrae winked at him.

Patrick Brannigan spat at Gallant, then again turned and began walking down the alleyway to give Dolan the good news. But he hadn't realized his mistake.

Marshal Liam Dolan leaped down from the plank walk, looked quickly into the darkness of the alley and saw a man emerging from the shadows, the glint of steel; the man advancing. He crouched, lifted his six-gun. Brannigan saw what was going to happen and yelled, 'No, Dolan, no!'

Dolan ignored the shout, or didn't recognize the voice. He fired four fast shots. Three slammed into Brannigan's chest, knocking him backwards. The fourth drilled a black hole between his eyes, but he was already dead. He fell into the heaped rubbish, his legs twitching.

'Dammed well done,' Gallant called. He rolled, came up on one knee and, head spinning, brought his hands together in mocking applause. 'The last of the fearsome bank robbers bites the dust, thanks to the courage of Dodge City's gallant marshal.'

Then he turned his head to the side and vomited.

Liam Dolan's eyes were adjusting. He took in the scene – Lancing motionless to his left, three men down in the deep shadows – and he walked up the alley. He stepped over Brannigan. Without a glimmer of remorse crossing his grim countenance, he looked down at McCrae. Then he levelled his pistol at Born Gallant.

'You didn't tell the full story,' he growled, standing with legs apart and braced. 'What about, "In a fierce gun battle in one of Dodge City's many back alleys, young Jericho Slade's English killer was gunned down by town marshal Liam Dolan."'

'Couldn't put it better myself,' Gallant said admiringly. Through Dolan's legs he could see McCrae moving. His hand had inched towards his six-gun. Now his fingers curled around the butt. 'You know, it sounds very much like something from the pen of Stick McCrae. You sure he didn't write that pretty speech for you?'

'McCrae's dead,' Dolan said, 'and you're next.'

'I don't think so.' Gallant shook his head. 'In fact, if you want my opinion, I think you're finished. I mean, how on earth can you come up with a story plausible enough to convince the senator of your innocence?'

'That's it. Enough talk. Say goodnight.'

Dolan's finger whitened on the trigger.

Stick McCrae cocked his six-gun and shot the marshal in the fold of his knee.

Dolan howled. He staggered sideways. The wounded leg couldn't take his weight. He went down hard against the draper's door, slid down it in a moaning, crumpled heap. His pistol was forgotten. Both hands, clamped to his knee, were slick with blood.

'You know, actually, I wish you hadn't done that,' Gallant said to McCrae, getting shakily to his feet.

'You got a death wish?'

'No.' He stretched out a hand, helped McCrae up. 'But we've got to present him to Senator Morton J. Slade as his son's killer. I don't know about you, but I don't feel strong enough to carry him.' He looked at Dolan, and grinned. 'Of course, we could always drag him down Front Street on his back – and across the railway lines of course – one man to each leg.'

'That sounds tempting, and it'd be rough justice,' McCrae said, 'but knowing what's going to happen I can tell you there's no real need for it.'

He was gingerly feeling his scalp. His hand came away bloody. 'A graze,' he said, 'but enough to knock me out and you know how scalps bleed.'

'What do you mean, no real need for it?'

McCrae grinned. 'You think Melody Lake, up there in her cottage, won't have heard all the shooting? Gallant, I'll bet you ten to one in silver dollars she'll be here, on horseback at the end of the alley, before we've dragged Dolan clear of that door.'

Stick McCrae won his bet. Melody arrived, Winchester jutting menacingly from her saddle-boot, looking her sparkling, vivacious best. Across at the stables they awoke the ancient hostler, and he grumpily supplied horses for Gallant and McCrae and an animal of a different kind for the marshal. They took Liam Dolan away draped face-down across a sway-backed mule. Five minutes later they dumped him in a moaning, bloody heap at the feet of an astonished Senator Morton J. Slade.